MURDER AT THE FASHION HOUSE

A 1920s Historical Cozy Mystery - An Evie Parker Mystery Book 8

SONIA PARIN

Murder at the Fashion House Copyright © 2020 Sonia Parin

No part of this publication may be reproduced in any form or by any means, without the prior written permission of the author, except in the case of brief quotations embodied in critical articles and reviews.

This is a work of fiction. Names, characters, places and incidents are the product of the author's imagination or are used fictitiously. Any resemblance to actual persons, living or dead, organizations, events or locales is entirely coincidental.

ISBN 9798642615201

CHAPTER 1

1921, Halton House

EVIE SET her fashion magazine down and gazed out of the window toward the garden, her look pensive as she said, "Poor Madame Berger. She must be feeling dreadful."

"What are you grumbling about, Evangeline?" the Dowager Lady Woodridge asked as she entered the drawing room. "I have come for afternoon tea, but if this is a bad time, I could make myself, dare I say it, scarce. There is nothing more disagreeable than drinking a cup full of woes."

Evie gave Henrietta a brisk smile. "Good afternoon, Henrietta. Do sit down, please."

"Are you sure it's safe to do so?"

"Yes, yes. It's quite safe."

"Well, correct me if I'm wrong, but something appears to have upset you."

Sighing, Evie walked over to the fireplace and rang for Edgar. "I'm trying to decide if I should cancel my subscription to my favorite fashion magazine or write to the editor. They have taken a stand against my favorite *modiste* and I don't care for the tone they employed. Nor their tactics. I believe they have decided to promote a new name. In my opinion, they are going about it the wrong way by dismissing one and favoring another."

"In other words, you are upset," Henrietta declared.

"My apologies. Did I use too many words to explain my state of mind? I have a cousin who is constantly accused of being too *wordy* simply because she enjoys speaking in full sentences."

"Did she attend your wedding?" Henrietta asked, her tone conversational. "I seem to remember meeting two of your cousins but they barely spoke a word."

"No, she didn't come. She had a bad case of the mumps. Otherwise, I'm sure you would have remembered her. She enjoys voicing her opinions." Evie guided Henrietta to a table by the window.

Henrietta looked around the drawing room. "Am I early or will it be just the two of us? I thought Sara said she would join us for afternoon tea."

"Sara made her excuses saying she needed to run an errand in the village, but Toodles should be down momentarily." Hearing the drawing room door open, she added, "Here she is now."

Her granny walked in saying, "I'm sure we won't look like the Bobbsey Twins now."

"What on earth is your grandmother talking about?" Henrietta asked, her tone hushed.

Seeing Henrietta, Toodles stopped in her tracks. "Oh... *Oh, heavens.*"

Evie pressed her hand to her mouth and tried to stifle her laughter.

"If you'll all excuse me for a moment..." Toodles swung on her feet and walked out of the drawing room.

Henrietta shifted and stared at Evie, her eyes wide with a mixture of surprise and shock. "I'm not sure I should ask."

"I'm inclined to agree, but then, what would we talk about?" Evie leaned forward and lowered her voice. "Earlier, my granny and I experienced a moment of disharmony and I'm afraid the situation has just been made worse."

The dowager could not have looked more astonished. "Did you have an argument with your grandmother?"

"Not exactly. It's just that she felt somewhat unsettled."

"By what?"

"It's difficult to say. I had been wearing a light green dress and Toodles had difficulty talking to me because, apparently, I was blending in with the sofa and she couldn't keep me in focus."

"Blending in?"

"Yes, and rather than cause her any further discomfort, I went upstairs and changed clothes." To Evie, that had seemed the easiest solution. "However, I made the mistake of choosing the same color Toodles had been wearing. So, when she saw me, she went upstairs to change." Evie suspected there might be more to Toodles' uneasiness. In fact, she might be experiencing the restlessness that always resulted in her sudden departure. "Honestly, it all begins to sound rather absurd."

Henrietta looked mystified, yet managed to say, "Yes, I agree, but why did she leave now?"

Evie raised both hands in a gesture of helplessness. "She'd changed into a rose-colored gown."

"Oh." Henrietta studied her dress. "But it's hardly the same shade. And what was that reference to the twins all about?"

"The Bobbsey Twins? They're characters from a series of children's books. They're always together and look alike and act alike." Had Toodles meant to suggest they had already spent too much time together and needed to have a break?

"Is she, by any chance, trying to send you a subtle message?"

"I'd just been entertaining the thought, however..." Evie's unladylike snort was followed by a burst of laughter. "You know as well as I do, Toodles does not employ subtlety."

"Well, if you ask me, your grandmother hasn't quite recovered from the shock of your triumphant return with that lady detective in tow. You completely derailed her plans to outsmart you."

"I'm afraid the consequences were far worse," Evie mused. "Toodles has now lost interest in becoming a lady detective." Evie wondered if that had snuffed out her usual spark. She would have to do something about it or risk her granny's visit being marred by unpleasant memories.

Evie continued by saying, "Now that Toodles has abandoned the idea of setting herself up as a lady detective, Caro refuses to speak to me. In fact, she hasn't said a word to me in weeks. You see, she'd had her heart set on assisting with investigations." And now, more than ever, Evie feared Caro might seek employment elsewhere.

The door to the drawing room opened and Toodles peered inside. Satisfied to see they hadn't been joined by someone else who might be wearing a gown the same color as hers, she entered.

Henrietta shielded her eyes. "My dear, you look positively resplendent in orange. Like a burst of springtime. You are to be commended. Not everyone could pull that shade off."

As Toodles settled down between them, Edgar entered, followed by a footman carrying the tea tray.

Evie watched her butler cast a wary glance around the room, his eyebrow lifted, almost as if to suggest he had noticed something amiss.

Her granny looked up and frowned. "Edgar, what is that odd look all about? You are supposed to inspire confidence, not cast doubt."

"My apologies, Toodles."

Hearing her butler use the familiar moniker made Evie smile. She hoped her granny overcame her restlessness and decided to once again extend her stay. Evie didn't think she would be traveling back to America any time soon and who knew if Toodles would ever return to England.

Brightening, Edgar walked past her granny and removed a vase of orange flowers that had been sitting directly behind her.

Noticing this, her granny gave Evie a knowing look. "See? I'm not the only one who notices these things."

Yes, but she was the only one Edgar made concessions for. Evie couldn't remember him ever rearranging a decorative piece just so she wouldn't clash with it. Or, heaven forbid, blend in.

"I will have to tell Caro to avoid selecting a green dress when we have afternoon tea in this room."

"You could always have the furniture reupholstered in a color you never wear," Toodles suggested. Tapping her chin, she glanced around the room. "There's an idea. I could throw myself into the task of refurnishing your house. Would you like that?"

Not in the least, Evie thought. Apart from a few modern additions, Halton House had remained virtually untouched for over a hundred years. She was only a custodian, tasked with the responsibility of maintaining the status quo and ensuring the estate remained intact and continued to flourish for future generations.

Evie scrambled to change the subject and hopefully offer a diversion. "I was actually thinking I would like to go into town and visit my favorite *modiste,* Madame Berger. I believe she could do with my support. But first, I think I will write to the editor of *The Stylist* and ask her to print a retraction. They wrote a dreadfully unfavorable article about Madam Berger."

"A woman editor?" Henrietta asked.

"Yes. Margaret Thornbury."

Henrietta lifted her chin and declared, "I think you

are within your rights to express your opinions, Evangeline. Indeed, if you do nothing, you risk being ridiculed by everyone who sees you wearing Madame Berger's creations."

Knowing Henrietta only meant to tease her, Evie ignored the obvious jab. "Then it is settled. Granny, would you like to come to town with us?"

"Us?" Henrietta asked.

"Oh, you must come too," Evie urged. "We must give Madame Berger our full support."

As the footman withdrew, he opened the door wider to allow Sara to enter.

Evie's mother-in-law smiled brightly. "I made it in time for afternoon tea, after all."

Toodles turned to greet her only to groan. Without a moment's hesitation, she surged to her feet and excused herself.

Mystified, Sara asked, "Did I say something wrong?"

Henrietta smiled at her. "That's a lovely dress, Sara. I don't believe I've ever seen you wear that particular shade of orange before."

"Thank you. It's called tangerine." Taking her place at the table, she asked, "Is something wrong with your grandmother?"

"No, nothing that a trip to the *modiste* won't fix. The sooner, the better. How does tomorrow sound?"

"I suppose I could do with a new gown," Sara said.

Looking at Edgar, Henrietta smiled. "Edgar. Could you supply us with pen and paper, please. I believe we must co-ordinate our efforts and draw up a schedule. If no one minds, I would like to wear blue tomorrow. Sara? Which color would you like?"

The door to the drawing room opened and Tom Winchester entered. "Ladies. Good afternoon."

"Oh, Tom." Henrietta clapped her hands. "Just what we need. A neutral shade of gray."

Tom approached them, his steps wary.

"It's all right, Tom. You're not in any trouble," Evie assured him.

Looking uncertain, he drew out a chair and helped himself to a cup of coffee. "I'm sure I walked in on something."

"Yes, indeed," Henrietta declared and proceeded to tell him about Toodles' obsession with not wearing the same color as anyone else. "You should be grateful, Tom. You don't have to deal with such petty concerns. Men seem to have it so easy."

When Toodles entered, everyone held their breaths. She hadn't changed her dress, but she now wore a light gray shawl over her shoulders.

Seeing Tom, she stopped. "Oh, for heaven's sake. Why are you wearing gray?" Toodles once again swung on her feet and exited.

CHAPTER 2

Later that afternoon

"Countess. Here you are."

Evie looked up from the letter she had been writing and wondered how many names she answered to.

The dowager called her Evangeline. Her granny always addressed her as Birdie. Her mother-in-law, Sara, tended to stick to Evie. And while the staff and everyone else Evie encountered addressed her as my lady, Caro wasn't addressing her at all.

As a fellow American and during his initial role as her chauffeur, Tom had addressed her as ma'am. Then, she'd encouraged him to break all the rules and call her Evie. Somewhere along the line, he had begun calling her Countess. It seemed to suit him. Surprisingly, it also suited Evie.

Evie set her fountain pen down and turned to face

him. "Tom. Yes, here I am. I take it you were looking for me."

"I'm only indulging my curiosity. Is something the matter with Toodles?"

"Oh, no... There's nothing wrong with her. At least, I hope there isn't."

"So why are we suddenly color coding our clothes? Apparently, I'm to wear brown tomorrow."

"Thank you for reminding me. I'll need to have a word with Caro." More like a one-sided conversation, Evie thought. "I'm not sure how she'll react to my request. She tends to be rather dictatorial about what I wear." Evie turned back to the desk and searched through a stack of papers. "Where did I put my color schedule? Henrietta is being highly organized. She has offered to inspect us all before Toodles comes down tomorrow. Apparently, we are to stand at attention at..."

"0900 hours," Tom said. "I was there for all the detailed instructions, but I missed the start of..." he shrugged. "Whatever this is. Henrietta tried to explain it but I still can't make sense of it."

Evie released a long breath. "Maybe there is something wrong with Toodles. Earlier, I thought she might have been feeling restless. You know she's always been active in one project or another."

"Meaning, she has always been busy trying to manage someone's life." Tom sat down and stretched his legs out and crossed them at the ankles. "It begins to make sense. She came here to manage you but you are entirely unmanageable. Now, she is at a loss."

"I believe you are onto something." Evie drummed her fingers on the desk. "A while back, she mentioned wishing to see her grandchildren aspire to something other than idle living. I'd been busy with something, I can't remember what, but I'm sure she threatened to cut me off."

Tom laughed. "As if that would make a difference to your circumstances. She must be feeling utterly powerless. I feel for your cousins. All unmarried and dependent on their inheritances."

"Oh. *Oh*. Do you think she will return to America and try to manage them? I'll be sorry to see her go and I believe Henrietta will miss her. Toodles has rather grown on her." Evie sprung to her feet and walked around her study. "Should we try to do something to keep Toodles here?"

"If we do, I think I will have to pay closer attention to my wardrobe and I'm not sure I can do that on a regular basis." He leaned back and stared up at the ceiling. "I might have no option but to hire a valet."

Evie stopped in the middle of the room. "Perhaps we could do something to engage her attention somewhere else."

"What do you suggest?"

"I'll have to give it some thought..."

The door opened and Edgar walked in. "There is a telephone call for you, my lady. It's the dowager."

"Which one?"

Edgar hesitated. "Henrietta, Lady Woodridge."

"How did she sound, Edgar?"

Edgar looked up and appeared to give it some thought. After a moment's deliberation, he said, "Slightly on edge, my lady."

"Heavens. What could be wrong?" Evie hurried to

the library. Before picking up the receiver, she scooped in a big breath and smiled. "Henrietta."

"My dear, Evangeline. I am in a state and close to asking for smelling salts, just like my mother used to do when she felt agitated."

"Heavens. Henrietta. What's happened?"

"I wrote down every detail for our planned trip to town but I must have been sidetracked and omitted to write down tonight's color schedule. What color am I permitted to wear to dinner tonight?"

Evie breathed a sigh of relief. "There are only three primary colors, Henrietta, and you claimed the rights to all the warm shades derived from red, including mauve, pink and violet."

"Are you sure I am permitted to wear violet tonight? Strictly speaking, violet is derived from red and blue and I think Toodles claimed blue and all colors pertaining to it."

Had it really come down to this?

Evie made the firm decision to contrive a plot to distract Toodles from her current obsession. Treasure hunts were all the rage...

"Wear pink tonight, Henrietta. I will make sure Toodles knows about it."

"Oh, but then that will ruin the surprise."

"What surprise?"

"My dear, Evangeline. One does not simply attend a dinner party. One makes an entrance. Why do you think we put so much thought into what we wear?"

Evie wanted to say she didn't put any thought into it because her maid, Caro, made all the final decisions about her wardrobe.

"Millicent has been taking care of Toodles. I will ask her to keep us informed. If Toodles decides to wear pink, I will let you know."

Evie returned to the library and declared, "Disaster averted."

"You don't sound so sure," Tom said.

She gave him a small smile. "I am almost tempted to leave it all up to the Fates. Let the cards fall where they may, so to speak. In fact, a part of me is tempted to sabotage Henrietta's hard work but as a hostess, it is my job to ensure my guests are comfortable." She flopped down on the sofa next to Tom. "Sometimes, it's hard work being a Countess."

Evie's gaze landed on her desk. Did she really need to send that letter? One person's negative opinion shouldn't really matter. Yet her sense of fairness intervened and insisted she had to do what she could.

"If you can't say something nice, then don't say anything at all..."

"Pardon?"

"Oh, nothing..."

Later that evening...

Evie looked at the pale pink dress Caro had laid out for her and frowned. "Caro, I'm sure I'm supposed to wear something yellow tonight."

Caro did not answer. Instead, she pursed her lips and lifted her chin.

"Caro, speak to me," Evie implored. "Don't you think this has gone on far enough?" Evie sat down at her dresser and, removing her earrings, she wondered if she should write a note to Lady Astor and ask for guidance. She would know what to do. Lady Astor had a special relationship with her maid. In fact, they were so close, her maid even traveled first class. Everyone knew about their animated arguments and there were even rumors of vases flying across rooms. Yet Lady Astor refused to part with her maid...

"You usually have a lot to say, Caro. Is there something going on in your life?" Evie thought of Caro's obvious disappointment in not becoming a lady detective's assistant, but what if there was something else disrupting her life?

Caro's face softened and she looked askance.

Evie decided her maid needed only a slight nudge in the right direction and she would cave in.

"I've been thinking... We might visit Seth at school. Although, that only leaves tonight to think about what he might like us to bring him. I know he loves cook's lemon cake but it might be too late for her to bake him one. I suppose we could pick something up in town. Oh, and some books. Yes, he'll definitely like some more books. Tom will help with that. He seems to have a better understanding of what Seth enjoys." Evie sat up and brightened. "Oh, I know. There's a store in town that makes the most delectable lemon drops. He's sure to like those."

"I have just finished knitting him a scarf," Caro murmured.

Evie could barely hide her smile. "He would love

that and you could give it to him in person." She watched as the edge of Caro's lip lifted.

Without saying a word, Caro took the pink dress and exchanged it for a mustard colored one.

"If you'll excuse me a moment, milady. I need to telephone the dowager and tell her not to wear pink tonight. There seems to be some confusion. Your granny is wearing pink tonight."

Had Caro been trying to sabotage the evening? Evie had just spent half an hour recounting the day's events with nothing but silence from Caro. She might as well have been talking to herself. Clearly, Caro had been listening and she had decided to stoke the fire, only to change her mind, all thanks to the prospect of a visit to the seven-year-old Earl of Woodridge.

Evie couldn't help laughing as she imagined Toodles entering the drawing room only to find everyone dressed in pink and all thanks to her mischievous maid.

Heavens...

She almost wished Caro hadn't changed her mind.

CHAPTER 3

THE NEXT MORNING, everything appeared to run smoothly. However, Evie knew appearances could be deceptive.

"What a relief. I see you and Caro are on speaking terms again," Tom said as they walked toward the front door. "How did that happen?"

When Evie didn't respond, Tom waved his hand in front of her eyes.

"Oh... I've been a million miles away all morning. As well as on edge. Honestly, Toodles needs to snap out of whatever has overcome her. She can't expect everyone to kowtow to her and cater to all her whims."

"Really? I've always thought she could and she does."

Yes, indeed. And, as a result, she found herself wearing yellow. Again...

"So, how did you mend fences with Caro?"

"Bribery, of course. I gave her what she wanted, more or less."

Tom laughed. "Ah, I see. You used Seth. I'm

surprised she isn't already married with a brood of her own."

"I think she dotes on Seth because of... well... everything that's happened in his life. She's like a mother hen, clucking and worrying about him. I suppose we all have our roles to play in his life." Evie slipped her gloves on. "I'm as ready as I will ever be."

"So am I. Then again, I only had to put on a suit and grab a hat. Brown, as instructed."

Evie glanced at him and smiled. "And, of course, you couldn't resist the opportunity to make a statement with your tie."

"I wondered if you would notice."

Evie adjusted his colorful tie. "To which Scottish clan does this tartan belong to?"

"I have no idea. Edgar helped me out. He has quite a collection of them and managed to find one with red, yellow and blue. Just enough to tease everyone."

"Making a stand, Mr. Winchester?"

"Someone has to."

"I suppose you think I'm weak."

He pretended to give the idea some serious thought then he smiled at her. "I think you want to see your grandmother happy. This is just a rather unique way of doing it."

Evie turned and watched the chauffeur standing at attention, ready to open the car door. With Edmonds already in London awaiting their arrival, another estate worker, George Potts, had stepped in as chauffeur and would drive everyone to the station in the Rolls-Royce.

Henrietta and Sara emerged from the drawing room and made their way out to the motor car.

As Henrietta walked past them, she gave them a whimsical smile. "You look quite pleased with yourself, Evangeline."

"I'm happy to see everything running smoothly, at last. Although..." Evie looked toward the drawing room. "Where's Toodles? We don't want to miss our train."

"She had Millicent dash upstairs to get her another pair of gloves. Toodles has decided to make a statement and wear blue gloves with her purple coat." Henrietta gave her blue sleeve a tug. "While she insists the gloves are purple, I believe she has managed to bend the rules in her favor."

"Why doesn't that surprise me?"

Watching the dowagers settling into the motor car, Evie tapped her foot, a feeling she'd forgotten something putting her on edge.

She heard hurried footsteps and a moment later Toodles dashed toward the motor car.

"Oh, I didn't mean to keep everyone waiting." Toodles waved her blue gloves in the air. "Tally-ho."

Evie and Tom stood on the steps of the front entrance watching the motor car pull away.

"Shall we?" Tom asked and whispered under his breath, "before you decide to send everyone to the lunatic asylum."

"Oh... I just remembered something..." Evie looked around for Edgar. "There you are, Edgar."

"My lady?"

"I left an envelope in my study. Could you please make sure it goes out with the post?"

"All taken care of, my lady. I noticed it last evening and sent it out then."

"Wonderful, thank you. Are you all set?"

"Quite looking forward to a trip to town, my lady," Edgar said as he opened the passenger door for her.

As she settled into the roadster, Tom gave her a bright smile. "You're really determined to make your point."

Evie shrugged. "On the one hand, I've been quite complacent and indulgent with Toodles, but on other hand, I believe I am making a stand."

On the train to London...

Evie looked away from the scenery whizzing by and caught Tom staring at her. "Oh, do stop looking at me as if I had just appeared from out of nowhere," Evie whispered and shifted in her seat. "You've been doing it throughout the entire journey."

"I can't help it." Tom adjusted his hat. "You still haven't told me what you wrote in that letter."

"That doesn't explain the way you have been looking at me."

"I'm in awe. The moment I have you all figured out, you surprise me."

"Says he who came to work for me under false pretenses."

"I still chauffeur you around."

"Only because my driving frightens you." Evie glanced at the dowagers and Toodles and caught them looking at them. The color coordinated trio did not say anything but Evie had no trouble imagining their inner dialogue. She leaned in and whispered, "They are bursting to say something about your tie."

"Stop changing the subject. The letter, Countess."

"Oh... I believe silence can be easily taken as consent and I could not accept that. Not in this instance. The author, a Miss Jacinta McKay, chose to promote an already fashionable dressmaker by denigrating another one. The fact it happened to be my favorite *modiste* hit a raw nerve. Surely there is ample room for both dressmakers to succeed. I might have mentioned something about her lack of scruples and maybe hinted at unethical behavior. In hindsight, I believe I should have written a letter to the owner of the fashion magazine. It's a woman and she ought to know better. Instead, I wrote directly to the journalist. I doubt that will achieve the desired results."

Henrietta gave her a small smile. "They say it is the privilege of mature years to find fault."

Tom snorted. "Henrietta just made you sound positively ancient."

"I believe Henrietta is referring to my wisdom and, hopefully, my rank, which should carry some weight. In any case, you could hardly call me mature," Evie whispered and thought of her granny who'd always encouraged her to remain young at heart.

"I rarely do," Tom replied, his eyes twinkling with amusement. "Although, you do a fine job of being responsible."

"Anyhow, I made it clear to the journalist I did not care for her tactics. I doubt their circulation will suffer if one subscriber cancels, but I intend to do all I can for Madame Berger."

"You could contact Martin Gate," Tom suggested.

Brightening, Evie searched inside her handbag and drew out a small notebook. "That is a marvelous idea." The newspaper owner had recently been on the lookout for a scandalous story. Evie wondered if she could entice him to write an article about the *modiste* and perhaps include a photograph of her latest creation.

"I thought your intention was to offer support, Evangeline. Are you now thinking of creating a scandal?" Henrietta asked.

"Certainly not. I would never expose the name of Woodridge to scandal but I believe it can carry enough weight to draw attention. It might be presumptuous of me to think anyone cares who makes my clothes, but you never know."

Henrietta leaned toward the window. "I believe we are about to arrive. Suddenly, I am feeling rather excited." She shared a smile with Toodles. "We are on a mission. How thrilling."

"Good Lord," Tom murmured. "This could set something off."

Evie couldn't begin to imagine what that might be.

"Is someone meeting us?" Henrietta asked.

Evie nodded. "Edmonds came up yesterday. We should all be able to squeeze into the Duesenberg. The others can make their way to the town house in a taxi."

Evie couldn't help noticing her granny's silence. She had barely spoken a word during the entire trip. Tapping her pen against her notebook, she tried to come up with a better way to engage Toodles' interest since a visit to a dressmaker might not be enough to entice her away from her broodiness.

"While we're in town I thought we might also pay Mrs. Lotte Mannering a visit," Evie said.

"You mean, Mrs. May Harcourt," Henrietta corrected.

"Yes, but as she introduced herself as Lotte, it rather stuck." Evie glanced at her granny. Mentioning the private lady detective her granny had hired to tail Evie only a short while ago didn't have the desired effect. Or so she thought...

Toodles huffed. "That charlatan."

Evie's eyebrows curved up in surprise. "I thought you liked her." Enough to engage her to set off in pursuit of them, Evie thought.

Toodles pursed her lips and looked away only to shift and huff again. "She's a fraud. What sort of lady detective is she when she couldn't even keep her disguise in place?"

"Here we go," Tom said under his breath.

"Granny, what on earth are you talking about?"

"Don't play coy with me, Birdie. You know very well you meant to crow, bringing her back like a trophy to show off your superior skills. If anything, you managed to prove me right. You are wasting your talents."

Henrietta's eyes sparkled with amusement while Sara looked on in surprise.

"In my opinion, you are the one wasting your talents, Grans. Yes, I think we will definitely pay Lotte Mannering a visit. I'm sure she'll be able to inspire you."

Toodles lifted her chin, her eyes brimming with defiance. "I know you are taunting me but you shouldn't be surprised if I do end up setting myself up as a lady detective."

"Just so long as you do it here in England."

Toodles sat back and closed her eyes. "I see it now. I could set myself up here and expand my activities. I might even rope in your cousins to assist me. They'd like that. Or, at least, Ruby might. She's a go-getter. I'm not so sure about Sapphire. She always has her nose pressed inside a book."

"Oh, Evangeline and Tom are forever buried in books, searching for information to assist the detective," Henrietta mused. "Don't you have another granddaughter?"

Toodles rolled her eyes. "Yes, the misfit of the family. Emerald. She's either poring through the fashion magazines, riding her horse or sauntering around the country club swinging a golf club."

Evie opened her notebook and wrote a reminder to contact her cousins and warn them of their granny's intentions.

Leaning over, Tom remarked, "Your dance card is filling up, Countess."

CHAPTER 4

WHEN THEY ARRIVED at the London house, Evie retired to her boudoir to change out of her traveling clothes.

"What shade do you call this?" Evie asked, her tone lackluster.

"Neutral, milady. A safe beige. You can't go wrong." Caro grinned and breezed about, happy as a lark, almost as if nothing had transpired between them.

Evie stood in front of the mirror and decided she would just have to avoid sitting on beige chairs.

"Are you sure you don't wish to join us, Caro?" Evie asked before making her way downstairs to join the others. "You could go as my distant cousin. That should be fun."

"No, milady. I'm afraid I have too much to do. I'm putting the finishing touches to Seth's scarf and I wish to visit a few shops today."

"That's lovely, but please don't go overboard. We want him to be happy but not spoilt."

Caro harrumphed. "I've heard horror stories about those boarding schools, milady. I believe he needs to be well-equipped and ready for any rising need."

"Equipped? With what? He has everything he needs."

Caro lowered her voice to a conspiratorial whisper. "Sometimes, bigger boys will bully younger ones."

Evie's voice hitched. "Is he being bullied?"

"No. But one never knows, milady. I believe I have gained his trust and he will not hesitate to communicate his concerns to me. So far, everything looks rosy. But, if we're negligent, we risk him being scarred for life."

Evie thought of the letters she received from Seth. They all reported on his progress and daily routines. He was excelling at languages, mathematics and geography but promised to do better in science. Thinking about it now, she realized he always employed a sense of reserve, suggesting he might have chosen Evie as the one person he needed to appease and impress.

At least he had found a confidante and Caro had clearly thought of everything.

Feeling a twinge of guilt, Evie dismissed it. No one in her family had ever been bullied. "I'm glad you're taking care of all the details, Caro."

"I haven't, not really, but we have Mr. Winchester to take care of the rest. During Christmas, he began taking steps to make sure Lord Woodridge can throw a punch."

Evie knew she should say something but she did not dare sanction the precautions being taken.

No one in her family had ever been bullied because

they had all been taught how to throw a punch. A solid one, at that.

"I hope you don't mind, milady."

"I'm fine with it all, Caro. Just so long as Seth is never the instigator." She adjusted her hat and smiled when Caro put it back in its proper place. "Is anyone teaching him how to make friends?"

"The sweets will take care of that, milady. Although, despite my concerns, from what he writes me, everyone wants to be friends with the Earl of Woodridge."

"Yes, I thought that might be the case." Evie turned to leave. "By the way, while we are in town, we'll be calling on Lotte Mannering." Evie did not wait for a response to the news. However, as she left the room, Evie thought she heard Caro do a little dance on the spot.

Walking along the hallway, she encountered Millicent dashing out of a room.

Seeing her, Millicent slowed down, bobbed a curtsy and hurried along, no doubt rushing to get the latest information from Caro.

Evie wondered if she might have to give serious thought to engaging another maid. After all, if her maids wished to seek adventurous lives she couldn't very well stand in their way.

"Ah, here she is. What took you so long, Birdie?"

"Last minute preparations. I have contacted Madame Berger," Evie said. She had also telephoned Martin Gate to ask if he would run a story about Madame Berger. She'd let him know they would be attending a preview of the designer's latest creations today and Martin Gate had offered to send a photographer. Evie had welcomed the news thinking a photograph of one of Madame Berger's dresses or even a photograph of them standing outside the building would be more valuable than an article.

Evie refrained from sharing this with them for fear they might think they needed to change clothes again. In any case, they were perfectly outfitted for an outing.

"Madame Berger has been quite accommodating," Evie continued. "Despite the short notice, she has organized a private showing of her upcoming summer fashion."

Seeing everyone turn toward Tom, Evie realized this might not be his cup of tea but she assumed he would find something of interest to entertain himself with.

"Don't worry, Tom. There will be plenty for you to feast your eyes on," Henrietta assured him.

The dowagers and Toodles made their way to the motor car. Following them, Evie leaned in and whispered, "There are some interesting shops in the area, Tom. I'm sure you'll find something to amuse yourself with."

"What? And miss out on a fashion parade?" Tom leaned in and whispered, "What if something goes wrong?"

"We are on our way to right a wrong. Why should anything go wrong?"

He shrugged. "Best intentions and all that."

Evie had no idea what to make of Tom's remark. He had been hinting at trouble on the horizon since they'd left Halton House. Should she take it seriously? Or had he meant it all in jest?

On the way to Madame Berger's Regent Street

establishment Evie found herself worrying. Did he think writing the letter had been a mistake?

"What do you think, Evangeline?"

Evie snapped out of her reverie. "My apologies, Henrietta. My mind's been drifting."

Henrietta gave her an indulgent smile. "I can empathize. My mind is constantly plotting out new paths for me. Anyhow, your grandmother has reassessed the situation and she is now willing to give Lotte Mannering the benefit of the doubt."

Toodles nodded. "She's in business so she must be good," adding under her breath, "just not as good as you seem to be."

Tom whispered, "Toodles doesn't back down easily. She must be up to something."

Instead of avoiding the subject, Evie met her granny head on. "Remember to tread with care, you know what the old biddies back home can be like. If they hear about you doing anything that resembles work, you'll be struck off."

Toodles merely shrugged.

Henrietta gasped. "Struck off?"

"Birdie is referring to the social registers," Toodles explained. "What do you think they'll do, Birdie? Ban me from the debutante ball?"

Henrietta laughed. "Forgive me, Toodles. I must be missing a vital piece of information. Do you do things so differently in America? Is there no age limit to a debutante's ball?"

Toodles snorted. "I attended my first debutante ball so long ago, I can't remember. Birdie is referring to all the dos and don'ts of society back home. They have some basic rules and high standards. Abiding by them doesn't automatically gain you entry into the snootiest circles. And those who are included live in fear of being snubbed and excluded from major social events and that includes attending the annual debutante balls. Working in any capacity is an instant black mark against you."

"Really? How odd."

"Why so surprised?" Toodles asked. "During my stay here, I have mostly encountered people who are free to come and go and attend one house party after the other without having to face any burden or obligation. I struggle to understand how they get by. Family money, I suppose. But the ones who do take up a profession are frowned upon. How anything ever gets done is beyond me. Anyhow, everything is changing now and that's why I am encouraging my grandchildren to make something of their lives."

"Oh, my. It's amazing how you managed to encompass so many opinions in one breath. But, you're quite right in saying everything is changing. We have become more tolerant and willing to move in tune with the changes."

Evie couldn't tell if Henrietta spoke with conviction or if she merely intended to steer the conversation away from disagreements.

"I believe I could pull it off," Toodles declared. "Yes, indeed. I could become the leading lady detective of my time. All the doors would be open to me. There would be no impediment. Just think, I could uncover criminal activities at the highest levels of society."

"Now you sound as if you're rather relishing the idea," Henrietta mused.

Toodles smiled. "I can think of several people who could do with being taken down a peg or two. I know where the skeletons are hidden and the bodies buried."

"Here we are," Evie said, her voice filled with eager anticipation.

The motor car turned into a narrow side street and came to a stop outside an elegant building in the heart of London.

Evie dug inside her handbag, drew out a card with the journalist's business address written on it and handed it to Edmonds. "That is our next destination, Edmonds."

He glanced at it. "Not far from here, my lady."

"Truly? Oh, do you think we might walk from here?" After the time spent on the train, she thought she might want to stretch her legs.

"Yes, indeed, my lady. I'd say it's only five minutes from here."

"We shouldn't be too long. I'm sure everyone else will want to return to the house after the show."

They were only a couple of steps from the entrance to the building when a woman stepped out, looked down the street and then headed in the opposite direction toward Regent Street.

A sense of recognition swept through Evie. "I think that's the journalist," she murmured and tried to remember her name. "Jacinta McKay." A couple of images hovered in her mind. The magazine often included photos of the writers. Also, she might have seen her at one of the many fashion shows she'd attended in the past…

Evie stood for a few seconds watching her and then

decided to take the opportunity to introduce herself. "I won't be long," she told Tom. Hurrying her step, she tried to catch up to the journalist.

Without looking over her shoulder, she knew Tom stood at the entrance watching her.

When the journalist reached the corner, Evie called out her name.

The journalist slowed down but did not stop. So, Evie hurried her step. She almost lost sight of her when she turned the corner, so she called out her name again and hoped Henrietta had already gone inside. Heaven only knew what she would say if she heard Evie calling out someone's name in the middle of a busy thoroughfare.

Jacinta came to an abrupt stop and swung around, a heart shaped locket swinging like a pendulum. With her fingers curling into tight fists, she said, "Lady Woodridge, I presume."

"Yes." Now that she'd caught up to her, Evie had no idea what she had wanted to say. She only knew she wanted to make sure there were no ill feelings. While the letter she'd written had been cordial she could not ignore the fact she had questioned the journalist's tactics and ethics.

"I wondered if you might be available for a chat later on. Are you headed back to your office?"

"If you have any complaints, it's not me you should be talking to," Jacinta snapped.

Evie could not have been more surprised by her tone. She didn't see any need to be rude.

Without saying another word, the journalist swung around and walked off.

Had she been referring to the article?

In all the time she had been reading *The Stylist*, Evie had never once read a piece critiquing a fashion designer, certainly not in a manner that would question the dressmaker's artistic creativity to the point of shattering their reputation.

"Countess?"

Looking around, she saw Tom standing by the curb.

"You look surprised," he said.

"That's because I am. Next time I find a bone of contention, I should remember to expect some sort of reprisal."

"I guess that means she wasn't pleased to make your acquaintance."

"I'm lucky she didn't throw a punch at me."

CHAPTER 5

"I suspect I might have caused some sort of trouble for Jacinta McKay. Although, I can't see how since I addressed the letter to her." Had her employer read it? "I think we'll play it safe and cancel our visit to her office."

"Didn't Edgar say he'd posted the letter last night?" Tom asked.

"Yes."

"Surely that isn't enough time for the letter to have arrived."

"He might have sent it by express mail. Or, perhaps I caught her at a bad moment."

Evie and Tom made their way to Madame Berger's atelier located on the third floor. They entered the elegant salon and were greeted by a young woman dressed in a pleated gray skirt, white blouse and black tie, her straight bobbed hair cut at an extreme angle and pointing directly toward her dimpled cheeks. Someone new, Evie thought as she didn't recall seeing her during her previous visits.

Evie hoped the tie wasn't part of Madame Berger's new designs. It seemed... too masculine.

"Lady Woodridge. Welcome."

"I hope this isn't too much of an inconvenience."

"Madame Berger was delighted to organize this special showing for you. The timing is perfect."

They were led through a set of double doors and into a large room furnished with velvet upholstered chairs in cream and gold. Evie looked down at her beige dress. Oh, yes. She would blend in perfectly.

As if reading her thoughts, Toodles said, "Birdie, stick close to Tom. Otherwise, I fear you might fade away."

"Thank you for the sage advice, Grans." Evie winked at Tom. "I hope this is not too dreadful for you."

"I feel quite privileged. I'm sure no man has ever set foot inside this palace of satin and silk."

The dowagers and Toodles settled down and became immersed in an animated conversation.

"We're anticipating the appearance of the first gown," Henrietta murmured. "I hope it's something I like. I fear too many choices will only trigger another debacle, with us fighting over who will get what."

Out of the corner of her eye, Evie saw a woman entering from a side door. Keeping her eyes lowered, she settled on a chair behind them.

Evie turned and smiled at her. The woman acknowledged her with such a brilliant smile Evie couldn't help instantly liking her.

Dressed in a stylish black gown with green trim, she

had a pencil poking out of her hair and lips painted a luscious shade of red. Evie did not recognize her and assumed she might be a designer working for Madame Berger.

When Toodles nudged her, she turned and saw the first model appear, preceded by Madame Berger herself who stood to one side and described each dress.

Evie didn't see a single flounce, frill or ruffle. Feeling self-conscious, she gave her sleeve a tug. It seemed she had become rather passé. She had only recently acquired some new gowns from Mrs. Green, a local dressmaker, who, despite making all efforts to keep up with current fashion trends, had obliged Evie by using her favorite fabrics and colors.

The model twirled and walked off. When the next model appeared, Evie's shoulders lowered.

All the clothes had straight lines and geometric patterns, the complete opposite to her favorite floral patterns.

While Evie liked them and thought they were perfectly suited to today's modern woman, she struggled to see herself wearing any of the creations. It seemed the fashion trend was here to stay.

Evie found herself sinking into her chair. Didn't she see herself as a modern woman?

She glanced at the dowagers and her granny. They all appeared to be captivated by the designs.

Did they see themselves wearing them?

They probably did. Which said a great deal about their generation. By comparison, Evie had seen few changes whereas they had gone from candles to gaslight to electricity. Surely she could adapt to dresses with no frills.

After the third model walked across the room wearing a dress in a geometric pattern Evie realized there would be no dresses in floral patterns so she turned her thoughts to her encounter with Jacinta McKay.

The journalist had recognized Evie straightaway. Had Jacinta seen Evie somewhere else?

Madame Berger held several shows during the year and most of them were attended by special clients as well as others in the fashion world.

Perhaps someone had pointed her out to Jacinta. She could well imagine how it had happened. Jacinta would have caught sight of a woman dressed in a frilly, flouncy skirt in a floral pattern and asked who in their right mind would wear such outdated clothes when clean, straight lines were all the rage.

Her thoughts meandered away and she found herself thinking how odd it had been to encounter the journalist coming out of the very building they had been headed for. Then again, there were quite a few fashion houses in the area. Perhaps she had been visiting someone else...

Evie entertained a few fanciful ideas, including one where she pictured Jacinta McKay receiving the letter and rushing to offer her sincerest apologies to Madame Berger, along with a promise to retract every single word in the next issue of *The Stylist*.

She then imagined the journalist being so angered by Evie's interference she decided to take it out on

Madame Berger by declaring she would ruin her and run her out of the country.

"So which one did you like, Birdie?" Toodles asked.

"Pardon?" Evie straightened and realized the fashion show had ended. "Oh... I rather liked them all."

Henrietta shuddered. "Some of those gowns seem to be missing a few layers. Call me old-fashioned, but I need my camouflage." Henrietta turned to Tom. "Did you see anything you liked, Tom?"

Tom cleared his throat. "There were some evening gowns..." He seemed to lose his steam. "I could see the Countess in all of them. I think she will shine in them."

"Nice save," Evie whispered.

"Actually, I'm not sure about the ties. Are women wearing them now?" he asked.

"I think Madame Berger would be only too happy to make adjustments for Evangeline. Here she comes."

The designer approached them, a bright smile in place. Slim, with an air of sophistication, she wore a stylish drop-waisted black dress with a single strand of jet beads.

As she neared them, her gaze went to the woman who'd sat behind Evie. Smiling at her, she nodded.

Evie felt the smile carried a great deal of gratitude. Had the young woman been there to offer moral support?

"Madame Berger. Thank you for organizing this for us and at such short notice too." It seemed unnecessary to mention the article or to even suggest it had prompted her to do what she could to offer her support.

Yet, by not introducing the subject, Evie felt she couldn't get to the root of Jacinta McKay's reason for targeting the *modiste*. What had inspired her to write the piece?

She had read other articles written by her. Jacinta McKay had always been fair in her appraisals, to the point of finding something she liked even when she didn't care for the designer's clothes.

Evie couldn't even tell if Madame Berger had read the article. If she had, she didn't show signs of having been affected by the negative criticism.

To Evie's surprise, the dowagers and Toodles jumped into action, placing orders and asking about a variety of colors.

Time to make a change and embrace the new styles, Evie thought and showed her full support by placing an order for one of everything.

"Including the ensemble with the tie?" Tom asked as they made their way out.

"I'm sure Caro can find something to replace the tie. I suppose we'll have to return tomorrow. Madame Berger has my measurements but Henrietta, Sara and Toodles will need to be measured." Turning to Henrietta, Evie said, "I'm glad you found something you liked. I feared some of those designs might be too modern for you."

"I thought so too at first, but I've had a change of mind. I simply adore those loose-fitting gowns. As a child, I remember having to wear layer upon layer of constrictive clothing; numerous petticoats, flannel in winter and stiffly starched cotton in summer." She sighed. "All quite cumbersome and torturous. Yes, I think this all worked out rather well."

"So why do you sound disappointed?" Sara asked.

Henrietta exchanged a look of amusement with Toodles that spoke of conspiracy or some sort of mutual understanding which excluded Sara. "I'm sure I don't know what you are talking about."

"I see." Sara gave a knowing nod. "You expected some sort of trouble."

Henrietta's mischievous smile spoke volumes. "I believe it pays to be prepared." Her lips quirked up. "I suppose you're right. Evangeline's letter and prompt action triggered some sort of expectation. In fact, I half expected Jacinta McKay to burst in and confront Evangeline. Oh, well, at least we have some new gowns to enjoy."

Stepping out onto the street, Evie glanced at Tom. "If I had to guess, I'd say you're wondering how women can make such a fuss about clothes." In reality, she knew he had to be on the lookout for a last-minute mishap. His focus seemed to be on their surroundings, a reminder that Tom still thought of himself as her bodyguard. As if anyone would walk up, snatch her right in the middle of a busy street, and hold her captive for ransom. She had not heard of any such incidents in England. However, there had been some cases of kidnappings in America, and that had been enough justification for Toodles to take action.

"Smile," Tom said.

"Smile?"

He signaled ahead.

Glancing away from him, she saw a photographer, presumably the one Martin Gate had organized.

"I think he's already taken his photograph," Tom said.

The man packed up his equipment and hurried away. Evie felt a flush of heat splash on her cheeks. "I hope I wasn't slouching."

"What just happened?" Henrietta asked.

"I think we have been caught in the act. What do you think the caption will say?" Evie asked.

"The Countess of Woodridge, out in full force, supporting her favorite dressmaker," Sara suggested.

Evie smiled. "Yes, that sounds good. Madame Berger will hopefully gain some positive attention from this."

Evie's cup rattled on its saucer. She leaned in for a closer look at the newspaper Tom was reading. "Wedding bells for the Countess of Woodridge?" Gaping, Evie set her teacup aside and made a grab for the afternoon edition of the newspaper.

"Countess. I'm shocked." Tom grinned.

"How on earth did that get in the newspaper?"

Henrietta smiled. "Evangeline, when were you going to tell us?"

"Yes, I can see how they arrived at that caption," Sara mused as she took a closer look at the photograph. "Caught from a slight angle, it looks as if you are tilting your head up to kiss Tom."

Henrietta's eyes widened. "In public, Evangeline, and right under our noses. I am speechless."

"Oh," Sara gasped. "Were you really kissing him?"

"Henrietta, you were there." Evie swung toward Sara. "And you were right behind me."

"There's no mention of Madame Berger," Henrietta

said. "Oh, wait. Here's something. The Countess of Woodridge hard at work ordering a new *trousseau*."

Evie yelped. "Who wrote that?"

"It doesn't say. Evangeline, it looks like you'll be writing another letter," Henrietta mused.

How could Martin Gate do this to her?

She looked at Sara and Henrietta. "I am so sorry about this."

"Why are you apologizing?" Toodles asked. "It's hardly your fault if you were caught in a compromising embrace."

Jesting aside, Evie had every reason to apologize but she knew her granny wouldn't understand.

Evie surged to her feet. "Excuse me for a moment."

Tom grinned. "Of course, dear."

Toodles followed her out of the drawing room. "Birdie. It's only a photograph."

"Grans..." Evie gave an exasperated shake of her head. "You know there's more to it than that. When I married Nicholas, I knew I would have to adapt to new responsibilities. It's a complicated life."

"Birdie, it's a life of privilege and adventure."

"You know what I mean. With the title comes responsibility. I cannot be associated with any gossip or scandal. The Woodridge family works in a caretaker capacity. They must maintain a sense of decorum and respectability..."

"It's just a name, Birdie."

"A name which has existed for a lot longer than any of us. We are duty-bound to do our best for the estate and all its tenants, the village, the parish... It's not just about me. I wouldn't mind that photograph making fun of me, but..."

"Yes, yes. I understand, but you need to step down from that soapbox you're on. You shouldn't worry about Henrietta and Sara. They're having a good laugh over it."

"I'm sorry, Grans. I must make that telephone call." Evie made her way to the library, her thoughts fixed on contacting Martin Gate and demanding an explanation, all to no avail because she couldn't get through to him.

As she disconnected the call, another thought intruded. In fact, it collided with all her other thoughts.

Her attention had been drawn to the photograph, but she had noticed something else.

"Oh, *oh, heavens*."

She swung on her feet and returned to the drawing room, her pace brisk, her eyes slightly widened as if she couldn't quite believe the image hovering in her mind.

Without saying a word, she took the newspaper from Tom and scanned the page. Skipping past the photograph that had brought so much unnecessary attention, her gaze shifted to the article sitting right above it. "Did you see this?" She turned the newspaper around and showed it to him, tapping the article with her finger.

"Ladies' fashion magazine columnist found dead," Tom read.

CHAPTER 6

Evie's heart thumped against her chest. "It's Jacinta McKay."

Tom's eyebrows quirked up. "It doesn't say that."

"It doesn't need to. I just know it's Jacinta McKay."

"You can't know that for sure," Henrietta said. "Her name is not mentioned anywhere. Nor are the details of the person's death. Indeed, we can't even be sure it was a woman."

Evie pressed her hands to her cheeks. A moment before she'd been sipping her tea and glancing at the newspaper Tom had been reading. Her gaze had wandered around the page and had landed on the photograph that had caught her by surprise, but along the way, the small headline had registered in her mind.

"Why do you think it's Jacinta McKay?" Toodles asked. "I'm curious to know if you noticed a clue that led you to the conclusion."

The letter she'd written, Evie thought. It linked her to the journalist. And, earlier, she'd had a brief encounter with her. She would be only too happy to be told the victim was someone else, but she had a strong feeling it wouldn't be.

In her mind, the connection had already been made.

"Countess?" Tom raised a querying brow.

"I can't explain it... exactly."

Henrietta shivered. "It would be an odd coincidence."

Sara agreed. "If it turns out to be Jacinta McKay, we might have to do something about Evie."

"Pardon?" Evie croaked.

Sara gave a small shrug. "We are living in interesting times. There are so-called spiritualists who claim to have direct access to the spirit world. You had a recent experience in that area. Perhaps there is a spirit guiding you toward people who might be about to meet their end."

"Interesting," Toodles said.

Henrietta snorted. "What nonsense. Evangeline is merely using her powers of deductive thinking and... and, well, it all adds up. Every time she has a clash with someone or some sort of curious interaction with someone, they turn up dead."

Oh, heavens.

"And that was precisely my point," Sara said. "We might have to do something about her."

Henrietta rolled her eyes at Sara. "Are you suggesting we lock her up in the tower room at Halton House to prevent her from inflicting her sorcery on all unsuspecting souls?"

Evie's eyes widened. "*Sorcery?*"

Henrietta patted Evie's hand. "I did not mean to imply you have some sort of supernatural power, my dear. I should have clarified that, but in the spur of the moment, I could not think of a better way of describing your ability to attract interesting incidents into your life." Henrietta glanced at Sara. "Is there something you wish to say?"

"Oh, I suppose you want me to apologize to Evie." Sara's eyes were bright with amusement. "You must admit it distracted you from the silly notion that you might have somehow caused this person's death."

"The thought didn't even cross my mind. Not really." Evie stared at the brief paragraph and felt incensed by the lack of detailed information.

Determined to find out all she could, she decided to make another attempt to contact Martin Gate. She excused herself and made her way to the library.

When she only got as far as his secretary, she pressed her for information. "Where might I be able to find him?"

"I couldn't really say, my lady. Mr. Gate left in rather a rush."

"Did he leave before the evening edition came out?" it occurred to ask. Evie interpreted the silence that followed as hesitation. The secretary knew something but, Evie imagined, she couldn't decide if she was free to impart the information. "Please let him know I wish to speak with him as soon as possible."

She returned to the drawing room and found everyone huddled around Tom.

"Could you all please stop looking at that photograph?"

"What did Martin Gate have to say for himself?" Toodles asked.

"He wasn't available."

Henrietta looked surprised. "I suppose he must be trying to avoid everyone keen to know if you have set the date."

Tom's smiling eyes suggested he was happy to go along with the joke.

Henrietta walked across the room and settled down at a small writing desk. "I shall send Martin Gate a note and request a copy of the photograph. It will look lovely in my drawing room. Oh, wedding bells. How thrilling."

Later that evening...

"Milady, everyone is talking about it," Caro declared. "I tried to dissuade them, but they wouldn't hear of it. I believe you have their seal of approval. Not that you would need it."

"Caro, you're not making any sense." Evie slipped out of her evening dress and handed it to Caro.

Studying the wine stain, Caro shook her head. "This is the last beige dress you brought with you." She looked toward the wardrobe. "All the other dresses will clash with what the dowagers and your grandmother are wearing. How on earth did you spill wine on yourself?"

Fed up with wearing beige, she had, quite accidentally, tipped her glass. "I have no idea. I must have been distracted."

"I don't suppose you would consider wearing white."

Evie pressed her lips together and gave Caro a hard look that only succeeded in making her maid laugh.

"No, I didn't think so." Caro rummaged through the wardrobe. "I suppose it will have to be the green one even if it is too glamorous for dinner at home. Anyhow... Where was I? Oh, yes. The staff heartily approve of the match."

Evie rolled her eyes, looked up at the ceiling and called for calm. "You know very well it was all a misunderstanding."

"Milady, forgive me for stating the obvious, but it is there in black and white."

"You know it's all a mistake."

"Is it?"

"Now what are you implying?"

Caro shrugged and looked away. "Only that you do spend a lot of time in each other's company. We were rather hoping something would come of it."

"We? Is Edgar in on it too?"

"Certainly not, milady. He would never presume to express his opinions." Caro grinned. "He merely shares them with Millicent and she expresses them for him."

Evie tapped her foot. Looking down at her shoe, she frowned. When had she developed the habit of expressing her frustration by tapping her foot?

What next?

A nervous tic?

"There must be a perfectly good explanation. I can't imagine what Martin Gate could have been thinking."

"He probably wanted to give you a little encouragement," Caro suggested.

Ignoring the remark, Evie finished dressing in silence.

Caro handed her a pair of earrings. "These will go better with the green dress."

"Thank you, Caro, but I really should go down and join the others. They have probably already moved on to the drawing room. I'm sure no one will notice if my earrings don't match my dress."

"I suppose so, milady. They are most likely too busy talking about the upcoming nuptials."

"You just can't help yourself."

"I'm sorry, milady. The opportunity is too good to miss."

"Yes, under normal circumstances I would agree, but I'm sure you've heard about the journalist's death."

"That's another reason why everyone is so fixated with your engagement. They really don't want to discuss the other matter. All the staff have said living in London exposes them too much to all this sordid business of people going around killing as if there hasn't already been enough of that. They see the wedding as a welcome reprieve."

Walking to the door, Evie stopped and said, "Caro, you should all feel free to enjoy yourselves, but please, I beg you, do not start talking about wedding cakes."

If the way Caro bit the edge of her lip was any indication, Evie would guess the ingredients were already being gathered.

As expected, she found everyone already settled in the drawing room. Unfortunately, they had not found a new subject to discuss. In fact, they were discussing dates.

"I always favor a spring wedding," Sara said. "That only gives us a short time to prepare, but as this will be Evie's second marriage, we can assume she'll be happy to forego the long engagement."

"She'll have to be patient," Toodles said. "Her family will want to come over from America and Tom will want some of his people to attend too."

They all turned to look at Tom. Evie thought he might shrug it off or laugh. Instead, he brushed his hand across his chin and said, "Summer would suit best with a honeymoon in Venice or Florence."

"Here's Evangeline. Perhaps she can throw some light on the matter."

Evie gave the dowager a brisk smile. "It warms my heart to see I can remain the center of attention even when I am not in the room." She moved toward a chair only to realize she would blend in with the green upholstery. Looking around, she searched for a more suitable chair. It happened to be across the room, closer to the fireplace.

"Birdie, how are we supposed to communicate with you? By carrier pigeon?"

One by one, the others joined her.

"I think we should play it safe and change the subject or risk Evangeline ostracizing us."

"Birdie can take a joke."

Henrietta nudged Sara. Evie's mother-in-law looked up. "Oh, yes... Hasn't the weather been wonderful. Not as cold as it usually is at this time of the year."

Evie turned to look at Tom.

He cleared his throat and looked around him. "This is a splendid room. It's interesting how you have grouped the furniture in separate areas. I believe I could spend an entire day here and not get bored. Yes, so many chair strategically placed around the room."

"Yes, we could all play musical chairs," Henrietta offered.

Glancing at Toodles, Evie thought her granny looked more cheerful than she had in days. Despite everyone's effort to change the subject, Evie couldn't resist the temptation...

Evie gave Tom a raised eyebrow look. "Caro informs me the servants quite approve of our match, Tom. Shall we set a date?"

Tom stilled. His gaze shifted from Evie and made the rounds. Everyone looked right back at him, their eyes filled with mirth.

"Cat got your tongue, Mr. Winchester?" Evie asked.

CHAPTER 7

Evie wished she hadn't given in to temptation...

Knowing any attempt to divert attention away from the photograph would be futile now, she told herself to grin and bear it as best she could.

Glancing at the clock on the mantle, she cringed. If she'd had an inkling of the havoc all this teasing would cause to her peace of mind, she would have organized an outing for the night.

With several hours to go before anyone considered retiring for the evening, she scrambled to find a different topic of conversation that would effectively bring the subject of marriage to a close.

She was about to suggest they play a game of cards when a footman delivered a message and Edgar stepped forward to announce, "Mr. Martin Gate."

Everyone instantly brightened.

"This should be interesting," Henrietta murmured. "Just when I was beginning to fade. I find this business of teasing Evangeline rather exhausting."

Toodles agreed. "We can now get the inside scoop."

Martin Gate entered the drawing room, his steps tentative, his smile apologetic.

The newspaper owner greeted everyone and responded to Evie's invitation by taking a chair opposite her.

"I'd just been making my way home from the theater when I picked up a copy of the late edition." He closed his eyes for a moment and then gave Evie a brisk smile as he offered a profound apology. "Of course, I do accept full responsibility."

"But how did it happen?" Henrietta asked. "Surely you're not saying you are responsible for composing the caption."

"No, indeed. My new editor..." He sighed. "As I said, I do take full responsibility. Needless to say, I will be printing a full retraction and apology."

Pushing for more information, Henrietta asked, "Did the editor take direction from you?"

Martin looked for a distraction and found it when Edgar offered him a glass of cognac.

Watching him take a pensive drink, Henrietta leaned toward Evie and whispered, non too subtly, "We might have to ply him with drink to get to the truth of it all."

Clearing his throat, Martin said, "I gave my new editor general directions. If you recall, my newspaper had been experiencing poor sales. Something had to be done and I did it by employing someone who came highly recommended to me."

"What exactly is your editor's expertise?" Sara asked, "Scandalmongering?"

Henrietta chuckled. "Heavens, Sara. Evangeline's upcoming nuptials can hardly be the cause of scandal."

Martin Gate tipped the glass and downed the contents in one gulp. Edgar, who'd been standing nearby, promptly offered him a refill.

"Thank you."

"I'm actually more interested in learning about the journalist's death," Evie said. "What can you tell us?"

"I'm afraid I'm not at liberty to divulge any information, my lady."

Evie looked at Tom and they both exchanged a raised eyebrow look that spoke of disbelief.

"In fact," Martin continued, "that is one of the reasons why I left the office so early. The police gave me strict instructions to keep quiet." He gave an apologetic smile. "I'm afraid I don't take orders too well. Especially not when I am in the business of reporting the truth."

Evie had to tell herself they were still talking about the death rather than the photograph.

"Why would the police insist on such secrecy?" Sara asked.

"I assume it is all part of their investigation," he offered.

"Evangeline believes the victim is Jacinta McKay."

They all looked at Martin Gate. When he did not react, Henrietta signaled to Edgar. Picking up the bottle of cognac, Edgar walked up to Martin, poured another glass, and then positioned himself directly behind his chair.

Martin gave his tie a tug.

Anticipating his next words, everyone leaned forward slightly.

"Yes... well... I can't actually confirm that... or deny it."

Henrietta straightened. "I'm going to interpret that as a yes." She turned to Evie. "You are to be congratulated, Evangeline. Your instinct was right."

Martin held his empty glass out and Edgar happily obliged by pouring him another refill.

"Who found Jacinta?" Henrietta asked.

Martin pressed the glass to his lips.

"Edgar."

"Yes, my lady."

"I hope we are well stocked with cognac."

"I believe we are, my lady."

"If she died in her office," Henrietta mused, "then, one can assume one of her co-workers found her."

Everyone studied Martin's expression but he gave nothing away.

"He didn't even blink. I am going to take that as a sign she did not die in her office." Henrietta turned to Evie. "Where else could she have died? On the street?"

Evie didn't think so. "There would have been too many witnesses. Far too many for the police to take control of the situation." Shaking her head, she said, "She obviously died in time to make the afternoon edition." Evie glanced at Martin.

Looking heavenward, he said, "Anything later than midday might not have made the afternoon edition."

"I see. Then, she must have died in the middle of the day. I doubt she would have gone home at that time, so we can discount her home."

Martin's gaze dropped.

"Aha!" Henrietta exclaimed. "I believe you're onto

something, Evangeline. She died in the middle of the day but not at home. Now we need to narrow it down until we find out where she died."

"Why is that essential?" Sara asked.

"Because..." Henrietta floundered. "Oh, because it will tell us if she came into contact with someone. If she died in the office, the police will be interested to know if she saw anyone out of the ordinary. Or, if any of the staff had reason to want her dead. If she died somewhere else, then the net will widen. There will be more suspects. Also, she must have died under suspicious circumstances, otherwise... Well, the police would have no reason to place restrictions on what Mr. Gate can and cannot publish."

Toodles clapped. "Henrietta. You have outdone yourself."

Henrietta laughed. "Heavens, I believe I have. Who would have thought I'd have it in me? Of course, I owe it all to Evangeline. It seems I have been learning from her through osmosis or some such thing."

"It stands to reasons she died at her office," Evie said. "But I can't think why the police would want to keep that secret." She glanced at Martin and noticed him averting his gaze. "Let's see... She's a journalist so she might have been out and about." Had she died at a fashion house?

The clock on the mantlepiece struck the hour. Ten o'clock. Madame Berger would be home.

Evie stood up. "Would you all excuse me for a moment. I need to make a telephone call."

As she made her way to the library, she wondered if Martin Gate had used the apology as an excuse to visit.

He must have known she would ask about the journalist's death. Since the police had prevented him from reporting the news about the death he might have felt the urge to somehow communicate the truth to someone.

If he had been intent on maintaining his silence, he would have stayed away.

Giving a firm nod, she decided he wished to be interrogated by them and pressured into revealing the details about the death.

As she dialed the number, she wondered how he had found out about the death.

A maid answered and explained Madame Berger had gone out for the evening.

"Did she happen to mention if there had been any trouble at her salon today?"

"No, my lady. In fact, she seemed to be in good spirits."

Ending the call, Evie paced around the small library and tried to imagine where Jacinta might have gone after their encounter. She could have visited anyone. She might even have returned to the fashion house. Heavens, she might have died at Madame Berger's salon and that would raise an obvious question. Why would Jacinta visit Madame Berger?

Evie remembered there had been a question of whether or not Jacinta had read her letter. Since Evie had seen Jacinta leaving the building, she decided to assume Jacinta had returned to her office. At which point, if she hadn't already read the letter, she would have read it and decided to confront Madame Berger.

"Yes, that makes sense."

Evie tapped her foot.

No, it didn't make sense.

If Jacinta McKay had died at the salon, surely Madame Berger would not have been in a happy mood. Then again, the death of the journalist who had denigrated her could have put her in a good mood.

She returned to the drawing room and helped herself to a cup of coffee. As she added some sugar, she asked, "Martin, how did you come by the news about the death?"

Before Martin Gate could answer, Henrietta said, "Surely you are at liberty to answer that. It's the least you could do considering how much embarrassment you have caused Evangeline. You owe her that much. Just give us a few hints."

"No need for that, my lady." Martin nodded. "We received an anonymous telephone call."

"So you did not recognize the caller," Henrietta mused. "Was it a man or a woman?"

"A woman."

"Now we're getting somewhere."

"Are we?" Toodles did not look convinced.

"Yes," Henrietta exclaimed. "At least he's talking. I think the cognac is doing its job. Edgar, pour Mr. Gate another drink. Make it a double."

"Did the woman have an accent?" Evie asked.

Martin took a pensive sip of his cognac. "Upper class."

Joining in the interrogation, Toodles asked, "Did she speak clearly or did she whisper?"

"The voice sounded strained and... Yes, somewhat

softer than a normal voice so she might have been trying to avoid being overheard."

"Evangeline, I assume you contacted Madame Berger. Did she have any worthwhile information?"

"She wasn't available but the maid said she'd been in a cheerful mood."

Henrietta conferred with the others. "Does that reveal anything of interest? Why would Madame Berger sound cheerful?"

Sara shook her head. "Heavens, we came to town to offer our support for Madame Berger, not to accuse her of killing her nemesis."

"Has any other newspaper reported the news?" Henrietta asked.

Martin shook his head. "That is what I find most frustrating. For once, I am first in with the news and my hands are tied."

That meant he had more details to divulge. "Did the police give you a timeline for this embargo?"

"Twenty-four hours to begin with, and they warned me it could be extended indefinitely."

What were they trying to do? Flush out the killer or protect someone's identity?

CHAPTER 8

The next day...

"Good morning, Edgar."

Edgar inclined his head. "My lady."

Peace reigned over the house. Evie sensed it in the air. Beyond the doors of the house... Well, she hadn't read the morning papers, so she had no idea what was going on and she didn't feel the urge to find out.

For the time being, Evie felt content. Caro had woken her up with a cup of tea and a chat about her shopping experience the previous day. The footmen she had passed on her way to the morning room had looked in good spirits. Glancing at Edgar, she saw him smiling. A good sign, she thought.

Evie helped herself to some breakfast and settled down at the table. "How did our guest settle in, Edgar?"

"As we assisted Mr. Gate up to his room, he sang a

ditty, my lady. So, we thought it best to move him to another room at the far end. I believe he is still asleep."

A happy drunk, Evie thought and smiled. "I thought I heard singing. You might want to contact his office and let them know he will be late."

Tom walked in. "Edgar. You're looking amused."

"Good morning, Mr. Winchester. I was just counting my lucky stars. It is a pleasure and a privilege to work in a lively household."

"As opposed to what?" Tom asked.

Edgar demurred. After some thought, he said, "Some households can be rather staid."

Sitting opposite Evie, Tom winked at her. "You are to be commended, Countess. You're providing your staff with lively entertainment." He arranged a napkin on his lap. "Where is everyone?"

"The dowagers and Toodles are hashing out their outfits. Apparently, they did not plan this far ahead. As you can see, I'm playing it safe and wearing a neutral shade. Not that I have any choice in the matter. And Martin is still recovering. Edgar tells me he broke into a song last night."

Tom laughed. "You have to give him credit. The man stuck by his principles until the last slurred word. If anything, we now know he can be trusted with any state secret. We'll either have to wait until his embargo is lifted or..."

"Are you about to encourage me to stick my nose where it doesn't belong?"

Edgar stepped up and offered Tom some coffee.

"Thank you, Edgar."

"You're welcome, Mr. Winchester. Are the eggs to your satisfaction?"

"They certainly are. My compliments to the cook."

Edgar nodded. "She'll be pleased to hear that."

Evie narrowed her gaze and aimed it at Tom. "Have you made arrangements with my butler to rescue you from having to answer awkward questions?"

Edgar straightened his shoulders and stared stonily into space.

"I believe you have hurt Edgar's feelings. You know he is devoted to you. Anyway, did you spend the night tossing around ideas?" he asked.

"I'm not sure how to take that." Did she have shadows under her eyes? "As a matter of fact, after I retired I spent some time writing to my cousins to let them know Toodles might rope them in to do some sleuthing for her and use the threat of cutting them off to stir them into action."

"It seems like a fair exchange to me."

"Yes, well... I'm not sure I'm ready to say goodbye to her just yet."

The door to the dining room opened and the dowagers walked in followed by Toodles.

"What's on the agenda for today?" Henrietta asked. "Are we paying Madame Berger a visit?"

"I suppose we must. Her maid would have told her about my telephone call and she is probably wondering about it. Also, she needs to take your measurements."

"Then it is settled. However, before we leave, we might have to reappraise our choice of clothing."

"What's wrong with what we're wearing?" Sara asked. "We're all dressed in different colors."

"Yes, but they're all the same tones. I feel we need more contrast." Henrietta stopped to inspect the bacon and eggs. "I don't wish to risk not fitting into my new gowns. I think it will be toast and tea for me for quite some time." She settled down next to Evie. "Is Mr. Gate joining us this morning or has he already staggered home?"

"You have a wicked mind, Henrietta. Poor Mr. Gate. I'm sure he doesn't usually imbibe so much." Evie looked up at Edgar. "When you telephone his people, you should suggest they send over a change of clothes."

"I shall do so immediately, my lady."

"There's no mention of the death in the newspaper," Toodles remarked. "I don't understand why the police are so intent on keeping it under wraps."

"Perhaps there's someone of note involved and they wish to avoid causing a scandal." Had Jacinta McKay annoyed someone else? "Given the steps they have taken, I believe we can safely assume Jacinta McKay died under suspicious circumstances."

"Murder?" Sara exclaimed. "Is that the general consensus? Did we agree on that last night?"

"Why else would the police become involved?" Henrietta reasoned.

"I don't care for all this uncertainty. If someone has been murdered, then someone needs to say it." Sara shrugged. "Then again, I suppose they have their reasons for placing restraints on the press coverage. As Evie just pointed out, there might be a prominent person connected to all this and we don't wish to see good names being dragged through the mud."

"And why would the police care about shielding this

prominent person?" Henrietta set her tea cup down and buttered her toast. "Their only job is to find the person responsible for committing the crime. If someone of prominence is in any way involved, then they need to face the consequences."

Tom looked straight at Evie. "You don't suppose..."

Evie shook her head. "No, impossible."

"I wouldn't be so quick to dismiss the idea," Tom said.

"What are you two talking about?" Toodles demanded.

"Tom is suggesting someone might have recognized me," Evie said.

Henrietta threw her head back and laughed. "I can see why you are marrying Tom Winchester. You can already read his mind and finish his sentences." Henrietta lifted her teacup only to set it down again. "Recognized you? Where?"

Evie couldn't remember telling them about her encounter with Jacinta McKay. In fact, she was sure she hadn't mentioned it. She gave them an abbreviated account and watched their reactions.

Henrietta's eyebrows shot up. "Did you deliberately set out to make a bad situation worse?"

Evie remembered Jacinta's reaction to the encounter. It had caught her by surprise. In fact, it had been unjustifiably abrupt. Evie thought her behavior could only be explained if Jacinta had read the letter. Even so, Evie couldn't see any reason for the journalist's combative reaction.

"I had planned on being diplomatic, but she didn't give me the opportunity to clear things up. I found her behavior odd. I've read many of her articles and I would never have thought her capable of such rudeness."

Edgar entered the morning room and made his way toward Evie. He leaned down and whispered, "I have contacted Mr. Gate's people. Also..." He glanced up and lowered his voice again, "Detective Inspector O'Neill is asking to speak with you, my lady."

"Speak up, Edgar. How is one supposed to eavesdrop when you go around whispering?" Henrietta exclaimed.

Evie surged to her feet. "Would you all excuse me for a moment, please. The police wish to speak with me."

Everyone's cutlery clanged against their plates. They all exchanged looks of surprise.

"I wondered how long that would take. Is it anyone we know?" Henrietta asked.

"Yes, Inspector O'Neill."

"Well, ask him to join us," Henrietta suggested. "We are like family now."

Evie's shoulders lowered. "Edgar, you might as well show him through."

Henrietta poured herself another cup of tea. "The suspense is making me thirsty."

The detective walked in and offered an apologetic smile. "I realize it is rather early in the day, my lady."

"I'm glad you caught us before we set off," Evie offered. "Do sit down." Evie signaled to Edgar and he promptly served the detective a cup of coffee.

As the detective helped himself to some sugar, Evie realized she had gained an advantage. Bad news could not sound so bad if it was delivered in a relaxed setting surrounded by the most important people in her life.

"I would like to think you heard about us all being in town and decided to drop in to say hello but I realize that is only fanciful thinking."

The detective looked at his cup and smiled. "I am here on official business, my lady. I only hope none of this gets back to my superiors. Then again, they would most likely expect me to extend the courtesy by not making this too official."

Henrietta looked at him, her gaze full of confusion. "Too official? How should we interpret that?"

Toodles piped in, "He's not bringing out the handcuffs."

"But surely Evangeline is not under suspicion, not unless the detective knows about the threatening letter she sent Jacinta McKay."

Evie groaned while the others stared at Henrietta. It took a moment for the dowager to realize what she'd said.

"Oh, do please disregard that, detective. After all, this is not an official visit."

The detective hid his smile by taking a sip of his coffee. Setting his cup down, he looked at Evie. "I see you have already put two and two together. Or did you, by any chance, contact Martin Gate?"

"Martin Gate? Oh, well... Let me think..."

Just then, the door to the morning room opened and Martin Gate walked in dressed in his formal suit. "Good morning. My apologies for wearing last night's clothes."

CHAPTER 9

"Detective, would you care for some more coffee?" Evie offered, her tone matter-of-fact.

Martin Gate looked undecided. Standing close to the door, he appeared to be about to retreat.

Tom got up to help himself to more food and, along the way, gave him a pat on the back and suggested, "You should eat something before you leave."

"Ah... Yes, I suppose I should." With a sigh of resignation, Martin Gate looked at the detective and gave him a nod of acknowledgement.

Settling down with more bacon and eggs, Tom said conversationally, "Martin dropped by last night to apologize to the Countess for printing that photo of us."

The detective instantly brightened. "Oh, yes. I saw it. I believe congratulations are in order."

Evie felt a deep blush settle on her cheeks. "Thank you, detective, however"

"Have you set a date?" he asked.

Henrietta's eyes brimmed with amusement. "We

were hoping for a spring wedding. But it seems we'll have to wait until early summer."

"My granddaughter is beside herself with excitement," Toodles offered. "Now she can barely string a sentence together. We spent last night talking of nothing else. Yes indeed, we only talked about the wedding."

"And yet, you all seemed to know the identity of the person found dead," the detective mused.

Toodles waved her hand. "Oh, that was nothing but a lucky guess. Where did she die?"

The detective's tone carried a degree of wariness. "In a fashion house just off Regent Street."

Toodles pressed her hands to her cheeks. "Really? You don't mean to say she died at Madame Berger's salon?"

"As a matter of fact, yes. Madame Berger contacted the police just before midday." The detective glanced at Martin Gate. "We arrived moments after one of Mr. Gate's newspaper reporters. Somehow, the press had been alerted at the same time, but Madame Berger swears she had nothing to do with it."

Toodles turned toward Martin and did a splendid job of looking shocked. "All that time you sat with us last night drinking Birdie's fine cognac and you did not mention a single word about it."

Henrietta hurried to say, "It must have slipped his mind. What with all that drinking..."

The detective's eyebrow hitched up. "You were in a state of inebriation?"

Tom smiled. "Drunk as a skunk and a jolly one at that. He enjoys singing."

"Like a canary?" the detective asked, his tone suspicious.

Tom shook his head. "No, like a drunken sailor."

Henrietta gave a vigorous nod. "We found it all quite entertaining. Evangeline had only just suggested someone play the piano when Mr. Gate broke into a cheerful song."

Evie sat back and listened in utter amazement as everyone delivered their fabricated versions of the previous evening with convincing ease.

The detective turned to Sara. "Lady Woodridge. Do you have anything to add?"

"Me?" Sara, who'd been occupied with buttering her toast, looked about and received several eye signals which she failed to interpret. "If you must know, Inspector O'Neill, we did try to get information out of him but he refused to co-operate. It seems you placed a ridiculous embargo and, true gentleman that he is, he kept his word and did not *spill the beans*."

"How did Jacinta McKay die?" Toodles asked.

Evie noticed this had been the second time her granny had managed to slip in a pertinent question.

"The cause of death is still to be determined."

That ruled out an obvious death such as a gunshot wound or stabbing, Evie thought. She must have winced because it drew her granny's attention.

"What are you thinking, Birdie?"

Evie shared her thoughts and added, "If the cause of death hasn't been determined the police might be looking at something suspicious such as poison. Jacinta McKay was far too young to have died from natural causes. Although... that is a huge assumption. Even natural causes don't seem to discriminate."

Everyone turned to the detective but he neither confirmed nor denied the suggestion.

"Are you going to tell us what brought you here, detective?" Toodles asked.

He turned to Evie and suggested, "Perhaps we should continue this conversation in private."

"Oh, there's no point in that." Evie smiled. "They'll all want to know everything and I'll only end up having to repeat myself."

"Very well." The detective drew in a fortifying breath. "Lady Woodridge"

Heavens! Evie hadn't expected him to sound so officious.

"Evangeline, whatever you have done, you have our full support," Henrietta declared.

The detective cleared his throat. "We have a witness statement from a person who claims she saw you having an altercation with Jacinta McKay in Regent Street."

"An altercation? When did this happen?" Henrietta demanded.

"When we arrived at Madame Berger's," Evie reminded her. "And, I wouldn't necessarily call it an altercation."

"What would you call it?" the detective asked.

"A misunderstanding. If I'd had the opportunity, I would have cleared it up but Jacinta seemed to be determined to stand her ground saying... Well, I can't remember what she said."

"Did you do or say something to antagonize her?" he asked.

"I can't be sure of that." Evie went on to explain about the letter.

"Ah, yes. The letter." The detective drew out a small notebook. Turning several pages, he tapped one. "Jacinta McKay returned to her office... Here it is. Her assistant says she had distributed the morning's mail and had placed your letter on Jacinta's desk. After reading it, Jacinta left the office in a hurry."

"And?" Henrietta asked. "Will you tell us the rest, detective, or do you wish us to fill in the gaps? We appear to be quite good at it."

"And she made her way directly from her office to Madame Berger's salon." The detective stopped to take a sip of his coffee.

Henrietta whispered to Sara, "He knows he has a captive audience but he chooses to draw out the suspense."

Instead of continuing with the story, he turned to Evie. "Can you tell me what compelled you to write that letter, my lady?"

Henrietta jumped in and said, "A sense of self-righteous indignation. Evangeline believes Jacinta McKay treated Madame Berger abominably."

The detective hid his smile by taking another sip of coffee. "Was there a history of animosity between you?"

Evie gasped. "Certainly not, detective. Despite what you might think, I do not make a habit of censuring the free press."

"But, in this instance, you did feel strongly enough to do something," he said. "Why is that?"

"Jacinta McKay has never before subjected a

designer to her harsh criticism. I believe there was malicious intent."

"You think she wanted to ruin Madame Berger?"

"She did not offer an explanation." Frowning, Evie tried to recall what Jacinta had said. "She might not have been responsible for writing the article."

It's not me you should be talking to.

Evie clicked her fingers. "Yes, I'm sure someone else was responsible for the article." Margaret Thornbury came to mind.

Had the editor forced her hand?

"Have you spoken with the editor of the magazine?" she asked.

The detective gave a small nod. "Yes, I needed to find out if you had made any previous complaints. Only because I wished to put you in the clear."

Before Evie could thank him, Toodles asked, "I assume you spoke with Madame Berger. Did you find her at all helpful?"

The detective gave the question some thought before saying, "The experience left her in shock."

"Surely she must have given you a detailed witness account of what happened," Toodles insisted.

The detective finished his coffee and set his cup down. "Upon her arrival, Jacinta McKay staggered and then collapsed."

"And that's when she died?" Henrietta asked.

"We assume so," he said.

Toodles got up and went to help herself to some eggs. "She arrived, staggered and collapsed. Did she say anything?"

"No."

"How can you be sure Madame Berger told you everything?" Toodles asked. "Did anyone else corroborate the information she gave you?"

The detective did not answer. In fact, his silence became an uncomfortable one and as it stretched, Evie wondered if Madame Berger had reason to lie or withhold information that might otherwise assist the detective in his investigation.

Jacinta must have been enraged by the letter. So much so, she must have decided to confront Madame Berger. Had she accused the dressmaker of influencing Evie into expressing her objections?

Henrietta picked up her toast only to set it down again. "I still don't quite understand why the police is so intent on keeping the public in the dark."

The detective reached for his cup of coffee. Finding it empty, he looked up at Edgar.

Instead of responding in his usual efficient manner and refilling the cup, Edgar looked away. It seemed the detective would not get his coffee until he offered an acceptable explanation to the dowager's question.

The detective brushed a finger along his forehead. "We have a new Superintendent determined to discourage the sensationalizing of news. He believes the detailed and lurid reporting of such events only encourages people to commit crimes in order to gain notoriety."

"What utter nonsense," Henrietta exclaimed. "We have a right to know. Indeed, I demand to know the details of every gruesome crime. How else is one supposed to take precautions? He cannot deprive us of something we have been indulging in since... Well, since forever."

Evie noticed Martin giving a small nod of approval.

"Mr. Gate," Henrietta said. "Do please back me up."

"I agree with the Dowager Lady Woodridge. The public has a right to know and newspapers have a duty to report the news."

"Not exactly the impassioned argument I expected but it will do." Henrietta signaled to Edgar who promptly refilled her cup. "Who does this Superintendent think he is? Has there ever been a public outcry over the reportage of criminal activities? No, I don't believe there has been. In fact, I'm sure there is a demand for more." Henrietta took a swift sip of her tea and continued by saying, "I remember my grandmother talking about the Ratcliffe Highway Murders and she would have heard about them from her mother who would have read about it all in the newspapers back in 1811. You cannot curtail something that has been part of our lives since... forever. I think I have already made that point. Repeating it only goes to show how strongly I feel about the subject." Henrietta gave Martin Gate a pointed look as if to encourage him to once again offer his support.

Martin cleared his throat and straightened. "The public have a desire to be kept informed. The dowager makes a valid point. You cannot deny the public's interest. In the 1840s, over two million people purchased a copy of Maria Manning's memoirs. She gained her notoriety by killing her lover and burying him under the kitchen floor. The interest was so great, Charles

Dickens attended her execution and used her as a model for his murderess in *Bleak House*."

Henrietta gave a firm nod. "It is simply unacceptable for the Superintendent to stifle the creativity of a writer. Who knows what stories could be written about Jacinta McKay's murder? What will we all do for entertainment?"

Everyone turned to the detective. Evie had never seen him so lost for words and she didn't blame him.

He gave a small nod. "I am well acquainted with the Maria Manning case and the Ratcliffe Highway murders. When the Thames Police attended the scene of the crime, they were accompanied by a swarm of sightseers. That is something else the Superintendent wishes to put a stop to. There have been far too many crime scenes disturbed and thoroughly contaminated by the general public. Also, publishing details about the incident can influence and even distort witness accounts."

Appearing to disregard the detective's comment, Henrietta mused, "Now that I think about it, murder is quite an enterprising business. The incidents are turned into fictional tales, they are retold in theatrical productions and performed on the streets and in puppet theaters. Or at least, they used to be."

Sara agreed. "Madame Tussaud's has several gruesome displays."

"At the end of the day, do we really wish to do away with crime?" Henrietta demanded. "Think about it, detective. You would lose your job. There you have it, detective. This Superintendent of yours needs to come to his senses."

The detective glanced at Edgar who continued to stare into space. "If you must know, the Superintendent's real objection is to some aristocrats going out of their way to seek celebrity prominence by employing rudimentary detecting skills."

Henrietta scoffed at the idea. Turning to Evie, she said, "Evangeline, I believe you need to put pen to paper again."

CHAPTER 10

An hour later, they were all color coordinated, in various tones, and on their way to Madame Berger's salon.

"Did Detective O'Neill say you were in the clear?" Tom asked.

Evie adjusted her gloves and turned to him. "Heavens, I'm not sure that he did. For all I know, he might have intended putting me under house arrest. I believe you, the dowagers and Toodles all managed to do a thorough job of derailing his thoughts. He left in a state of utter confusion. In fact, I wouldn't be surprised if he's right this minute scratching his head and wondering what happened."

The detective hadn't said who had identified her. Evie didn't remember seeing anyone on the street she recognized. Although, at the time, her focus had been on catching up with Jacinta McKay. If she had been spotted by one of her peers, why would they contact the police? To Evie, it felt like an act of betrayal.

"You look worried," Tom said.

"I am." She gave a small shrug. "I'm not that prominent, yet someone saw me approaching Jacinta and they told the police. Not only that, they said I'd been involved in an altercation. You were watching me. Did it look to you as if we were arguing?"

"I could only see your back and, at one point, you took a small step back. I imagine you were gaping at the time. In my opinion, you were on the defensive."

Yes, and Jacinta had been on the offensive...

If she'd insisted on knowing, would the detective have revealed the identity of his informer? She didn't think so. "Did you notice anything odd about the detective?"

"I think he might have been experiencing an inner struggle. He must be under a lot of pressure. It can't be easy dealing with a new Superintendent determined to make a difference," Tom said. "Especially when the task falls on the detective to enforce the new rules."

Evie agreed and, while the detective hadn't made it perfectly clear, she knew he would advise against becoming involved in the case.

Listening to Toodles and the dowagers discuss the little information the detective had shared with them, Evie thought about their obvious fascination with the murder case.

As Henrietta had pointed out, the public's interest in such news was not exactly new. Evie decided it had somewhat increased since the war. When she shared her thoughts, everyone agreed.

"Yet Caro told me the household staff have had enough of violence."

"Nonsense. They only say that because they are currently entertained by your marriage plans. Give them a few days and they'll be turning the pages of the newspapers looking for news about the murder." Henrietta tipped her head and struck up a pensive pose. "I do believe we wish to be entertained. You know, murder games have become all the rage."

Henrietta's remark silenced everyone into introspection.

Evie couldn't decide if she agreed about the appeal of murders or not. After the misery everyone had experienced during the war, she would have assumed everyone simply wanted to get on with it. Was she wrong in thinking that? Had everyone recovered their sense of intrigue?

She wondered what the effects of ongoing exposure to detailed reporting of murders would have on people. Would they become insouciant and less likely to respond with shuddering horror the way they had to news about the war?

When they arrived at their destination Toodles asked, "Do we have a plan?"

"I would like answers," Henrietta declared. "I believe Madame Berger withheld some vital information."

"Deliberately?" Sara asked.

"We should give her the benefit of the doubt," Evie said. "After all, she suffered a great shock." Shrugging, she added, "The detective knows how to perform his duty. If Madame Berger failed to reveal all she knows, he will get to the bottom of it. Although, he doesn't have our advantage..."

"And what might that be?" Toodles asked.

"Asking questions that might not otherwise occur to him."

Tom laughed. "That's because the detective relies on common sense and years of experience."

Evie gaped at him. "Are you suggesting we don't have any common sense?"

Tom put both hands up. "My apologies. Your unique approaches have been quite effective in gaining results. Even your reluctance to become involved has worked in your favor."

They made their way to the salon and were greeted by the receptionist who said, "I'll let Madame Berger know you are here."

Watching the receptionist making her way down a hallway, Evie remembered what she'd said the previous day.

Perfect timing...

What had she meant? Perfect timing because they were all set up to display their gowns or perfect timing because their arrival suited their purposes in other ways?

Hearing footsteps approaching, they all fell silent.

Madame Berger welcomed them and showed them through to a small elegantly appointed drawing room.

Looking in fine spirits, almost as if nothing had happened, Madame Berger promptly organized a couple of assistants to start taking measurements.

As the dowagers and Toodles were ushered to a fitting room area, Evie and Tom were encouraged to make themselves comfortable on a couple of chairs placed near a fireplace.

Evie looked around the room. Apart from thick velvet curtains, there were no other decorations. Nothing to distract her thoughts, which should have been the perfect moment for her to focus on the questions she needed to ask.

Belatedly, Evie wished Toodles had remained behind. She seemed to be the only one asking the right questions.

"We heard about the dreadful incident," Tom said.

Evie watched Madame Berger's reaction only to be disappointed to see her stare blankly at Tom.

"Lady Woodridge and I were actually surprised to find your establishment open for business," Tom added.

Once again, Evie found someone else making a leading remark. Had she lost her touch?

"I have many people relying on me," Madame Berger finally said, her French accent slipping slightly, triggering Evie's suspicion Madame Berger didn't possess a single drop of French blood.

While her casual response should have struck her as odd, it didn't. Evie understood the need for pretense. Although, she never really thought of it in those terms. Rather, it was all about putting one's best foot forward regardless of how one felt. As a businesswoman, Madame Berger would want to and need to just carry on.

When she turned to Evie, her expression lacked any telltale signs of emotion. "I understand you telephoned last night. My apologies for not being available, my lady. I'd had a previous engagement I could not get out of. Otherwise, I would not have thought of going out after that dreadful tragedy."

"Do you know why Jacinta McKay came to visit you?" Tom asked.

"I'm not entirely sure. She wrote for a leading fashion magazine, so I assume she wished to write something."

That surprised Evie. Did it mean Madame Berger had not read the article?

"Oh," Tom looked at Evie and then at Madame Berger. "So, you didn't read the article she wrote about your latest creations."

Madame Berger stiffened her back and pursed her lips. A sure sign she knew all about the article.

Evie waited for the denial to come.

"No, I had not been aware of it."

But she was aware of it now?

While any other person might have asked questions, she didn't show the slightest interest in learning more.

Evie went through everything the detective had told them and wondered if someone else had witnessed the death. Otherwise, he would have to take Madame Berger's word, and that didn't seem to be that reliable.

Beating her to the question, Tom asked, "Was anyone else present when Jacinta McKay arrived?"

"Yes. Louisa Barclay. She is a new designer. I have taken her under my wing. In fact, she has a salon in this very building."

Evie had never heard of her.

"You might have noticed her," Madame Berger said. "She was here yesterday."

"Oh," Evie exclaimed. "The young woman sitting in the back."

"Yes, that's right."

Did the detective know that? Evie straightened and leaned forward. However, Tom managed to snatch the words before she could even open her mouth.

"Did you tell Detective O'Neill about her?" Tom asked.

"It didn't come up." Madame Berger's gaze jumped between them. "I am still in shock. In fact, I could not speak for several minutes."

"So, who contacted the police?" Tom asked.

"I... I'm not sure. I suppose one of the assistants."

In her hurry to say something relevant, Evie's voice hitched. "Could you find out?"

Startled, Madame Berger jumped back. "Y-yes. Certainly. But I don't understand why you would wish to know." As she hurried away, she glanced over her shoulder, her eyes slightly wide with shock.

"You cracked the whip," Tom said.

"I didn't mean to. Every time I wished to ask a pertinent question, you beat me to it."

Tom winked at her. "Maybe Henrietta is right and we are able to read each other's thoughts."

Evie looked toward the door. "I wonder if she really went in search of answers or if she just wanted to avoid an uncomfortable situation. Then again... I shouldn't be asking any questions. It's not my job."

Again, Tom laughed, "Strictly speaking, you haven't been asking any questions."

Evie leaned in and whispered, "Do you think she's been honest with us? She just lied about not being the one who contacted the police. Jacinta died here, so she must have been the one to alert the authorities. In fact, I'm sure that's what the detective said."

Tom gave a slow shake of his head. "Honest? No, not for a moment. I certainly don't believe she didn't read the article. It's her business to be informed."

So, what could she be hiding?

Evie tried to picture the scene. Even if she'd been in shock, surely, she would have snapped out of it long enough to take command of the situation.

Turning, she saw the young woman who had greeted them at the door. She wore head to toe black, including a black tie.

She set a tray down on a small table and poured some tea.

"I suppose keeping busy helps," Tom said, his tone conversational.

The young woman nodded, the slight frown on her forehead disappearing as she straightened.

"What's your name?"

"Lucy."

Tom held her gaze for a moment. "Lucy, we've just been talking about Jacinta McKay. Did you see what happened?"

Lucy looked over her shoulder and lowered her voice to say, "It was dreadful. Jacinta McKay just rolled her eyes back and collapsed."

"And she didn't say anything?" Tom asked.

"No. I met her at reception and she just staggered right past me."

"And where was Madame Berger?"

"Standing by the door to this room. She went pale. For a moment, I thought she might collapse too."

"But then, she recovered and contacted the police and the newspaper."

Lucy glanced over her shoulder. "No, she... She didn't call anyone."

Hearing footsteps approaching, Lucy stepped away. "I should go." Lucy rushed out another door and closed it behind her.

Madame Berger walked in. She looked quite pleased with herself, suggesting she might have had some success. "Mystery solved. My assistant, Lucy, alerted the police."

Interesting, Evie thought. Why had Madame Berger lied again?

Evie lifted the cup to her lips only to set it down again as she remembered they were dealing with a poisoner on the loose. "I understand Jacinta McKay visited you at midday."

Madame Berger gave a cautious nod.

"Did she visit you earlier?"

"I'm not sure what you mean, my lady."

"As we entered the building, she was coming out," Evie explained.

Madame Berger shrugged. "It's possible she visited someone else in the building. Mine is not the only fashion house here."

The dowagers and Toodles emerged from an adjoining room smiling and chatting.

"Evangeline, thank you for suggesting this. I had so much fun."

"Birdie, did you need to have yourself measured?"

Evie looked down at her cream-colored drop-waisted silk dress. All her gowns felt suitably loose and comfortable. Did Toodles think she had gained weight?

"Oh, I'm only teasing, Birdie. And your expression was priceless."

When they all laughed, Evie jumped to her feet. "Yes, well... I could do with a cup of tea. The Ritz, anyone? They put on a wonderfully enticing spread."

Henrietta nudged Toodles. "I believe Evangeline is now teasing us."

CHAPTER 11

"I WOULD APPRECIATE it if everyone would please refrain from ordering anything caked in temptation. I must be able to fit into my new gowns," Henrietta exclaimed as they made their way to the Palm Court.

Toodles laughed. "You know Birdie brought us here on purpose but I think the joke is on her. I've never seen so much cream-colored furniture. We should sit somewhere near a palm tree so she doesn't blend in and fade away."

"I might have to start wearing black," Evie whispered.

Hearing her, Henrietta laughed. "Evangeline, there's no need for such extreme action. I believe hair dying is becoming fashionable. Have you considered changing the color of your hair? That's not to say I agree with your grandmother's insinuation that you've been blending in. You have too much presence for that to ever happen."

Settling down at a round table, Evie drew out a small notebook and began jotting down some facts.

"What is Madame Berger hiding?" Tom read.

Evie tapped her pen on the notebook. "She pretended she didn't know about the inflammatory article so we can assume she doesn't wish the police to think that might be a motive for murder."

"Does this mean you will investigate?" Toodles asked.

"Certainly not. Now that we have the gowns all organized, we have to think about making our way to visit Seth. I'm sure Caro said she had everything ready."

"So why are you taking notes?"

"Force of habit."

"You can't just hold on to the information," Toodles said. "You must share it with the detective."

"Yes, I agree," Henrietta offered.

Evie looked at Sara.

"Oh, I suppose I agree too. After all, he's only responsible for enforcing the embargo. It's not his fault he has a Superintendent who is out of touch. Yes, you should help him."

"When you contact him," Toodles said, "Tell him Madame Berger is definitely lying. She has copies of the magazine in the fitting rooms. And the young girl who took my measurements talked of nothing else. Apparently, Madame Berger lost her temper when she read the article."

"Did she make any threats?" Evie asked only to put her hand up. "No, no. Don't tell me. I'll pass on whatever information I have to the detective. It will be up to him to do his job."

When she finished writing her notes, she picked up the menu and pretended to study it. In reality, her thoughts were fixated on Madame Berger's lies.

Detective O'Neill had asked if she'd had a history of animosity with Jacinta McKay. Had he asked Madame Berger the same question? He must have, Evie thought. And she guessed Madame Berger had given a misleading answer. In fact, the designer had probably pretended to have been the best of friends with Jacinta.

What if something had happened between them? Evie thought they might have argued, resulting in Jacinta taking up arms against Madame Berger.

Feeling frustrated by the lack of information, Evie set her menu down. "Unless anyone can think of a reason why we should remain in town, I propose setting off tomorrow." That would take care of the temptation to delve into matters that did not concern her.

To her surprise, the dowagers and Toodles suddenly found reasons to remain in town for another couple of days.

"Oh, my dear Evangeline, I don't mean to disrupt your plans but spring is here and I'm sure I could do with a new hat or maybe two. Yes, a visit to my milliner should take care of that and I might as well see to it now otherwise I'll think of a dozen reasons why I shouldn't get another hat. After all, I am getting on in age and..." Henrietta turned to Sara, her eyes communicating a desire for support.

"A new hat sounds like a splendid idea," Sara piped in. "I had just been entertaining the same thought."

Toodles smiled. "You can never have too many hats.

Specially for Sunday service. I noticed the locals seem to take great pleasure in seeing what we wear."

Evie turned to Tom. "I suppose you need a new hat too."

Their morning refreshments turned into a light lunch filled with suppositions and conspiracies. When they returned to the house Evie was only too happy to enjoy some peace and quiet in the library. Although, it didn't last…

Tom finished reading his newspaper and set it aside next to the stack of other newspapers he'd already read. "Wouldn't it be easier to telephone the detective?"

"I'm nearly finished." Evie stopped in mid-sentence and looked out the window. She had kept the missive short and to the point, all the while thinking she was providing superfluous information. By now, she thought, the detective must have collected the same information and reached the same conclusions.

Madame Berger was hiding something. Her guilt, Evie thought.

For all she knew, the detective had already uncovered a web of deceit and might even be right that minute in the process of taking the woman into custody.

Evie tapped her foot. Noticing this, she growled softly under her breath.

"Do you need help remembering the details?" Tom asked.

"No, I'm just trying to figure out how to get this

note to the detective. Posting it seems too nonchalant. There might be a small chance the letter contains vital information which should reach the detective as soon as possible."

"You could hand deliver it, but that would defeat the purpose of trying to keep your distance."

Evie slipped the note inside an envelope and addressed it to Inspector O'Neill.

Turning, she saw Tom surrounded by newspapers and magazines. "You have been busy reading. Strange. I noticed that a couple of minutes ago, but the thought only now registered in my mind." How long had she been writing her letter?

"Yes, I found these magazines stacked in a corner. Would you believe I came across several articles written about Lotte Mannering?"

She glanced over at the magazines and identified them as some her granny had brought on her last visit to her. "No, I don't believe it. Does she advertise her services in America too?" They had recently seen some advertisements for her services and had also discovered she was in competition with another lady detective.

"She certainly does. In fact, she has been a regular traveler to both Europe and America." He leaned over and picked up one of the magazines. "In this one, she explains why she often disguises herself as a man. Apparently, women cannot stand about the way men can."

"How ludicrous. How can you become suspicious just because you happen to stand in place for longer than a minute?"

Tom agreed. "I would be riled too at the suggestion

a woman is up to no good simply because she doesn't wish to move. I'm almost tempted to put it to the test and see what happens." He set the magazine down. "Do you think I'd be propositioned?"

"It depends on how good your disguise is. Then again, you might attract attention for entirely the wrong reasons. We seem to be living in interesting times."

Evie turned and picked up the envelope. Not sharing the information with the detective would be irresponsible but she had to find a way to get it to him without appearing to be taking an active interest in the case.

She looked up at the clock. Afternoon tea wouldn't be for quite a while. If she was going to deliver the letter, she should do it soon.

Sitting back, she closed her eyes and tried to think if she had left anything out. In her opinion, there were quite a few questions which needed answers. If the detective hadn't thought to address those questions, she thought he should at least be aware of them.

Why had Jacinta McKay visited Madame Berger after writing such a dreadful article about her designs? More importantly, had the magazine owner directed her to write the article?

Evie drummed her fingers on the desk. She knew she'd started going around in circles so she tried to find something else to think about.

"Countess? Is something on your mind?"

"Yes. I've been trying to distract myself but the thought refuses to let go. Margaret Thornbury."

"The magazine owner?"

"Yes." Evie bit the edge of her lip. "I know I said I wouldn't prod for answers however, I don't see what harm it would do to speak with her. Only as a matter of curiosity and not because I'm delving."

Giving her his full attention, Tom set aside the magazine he'd just picked up. "Are you trying to justify paying her a visit?"

"I have no business going to see her."

"Would you like me to provide you with an excuse?" Tom asked.

"It would have to be a solid one. Something that would stand up in a court of law. I really don't wish to get on the detective's bad side. I'm sure he has one."

"If the detective ever finds out you visited Margaret Thornbury, you could say you wished to express your condolences. Of course, Margaret Thornbury isn't directly related to the victim, but I'm sure all the staff at the magazine experienced a shock. Sensitive and well-meaning person that you are, you want to offer your moral support."

Evie gave him a bright smile. "You're rather good at this." Jumping to her feet, she walked across the room and pulled the bell cord. If they were going to do this, she thought it would be best to do it without an entourage.

When Edgar appeared, she said, "Edgar, if anyone asks you about our whereabouts, you can say Mr. Winchester and I went out to see if we can find some books for Seth."

Edgar cleared his throat. "Will I be covering for you, my lady? I only ask because Toodles is likely to press me for more information. In which case, I might need to employ my creativity."

"Feel free to use whatever means you feel are necessary, Edgar." She didn't wish to be forced to explain her actions to her granny who would no doubt ask why she'd wanted to speak to the magazine owner. "If nothing comes to mind, you can say we have also gone out in search of a new hat for Mr. Winchester."

※

They found *The Stylist* magazine office located only a few minutes away from Madame Berger's salon.

Adjusting her gloves, Evie leaned forward. "Edmonds, we shouldn't be too long."

Her chauffeur tipped his cap and sat back to read the newspaper.

That reminded Evie about Martin Gate's assurance. Had he printed a retraction?

Stepping out of the motor car, she smiled up at Tom. "You're not a happy back seat driver."

"What gave me away?"

"You gritted your teeth all the way here."

Tom's uncharacteristic moan expressed his feelings only too clearly. "I miss the roadster."

They both turned and looked up at the buff colored Georgian building with a sunken basement. Quite typical of residential houses in town, Evie thought. In fact, it was a smaller version of the one she owned.

"Are you sure this is the right address?" Tom asked.

Evie looked up and down the street. Next door, she

saw a residential entrance and beyond that, an exclusive milliner's store.

"I copied the address straight from the magazine. I assume they must have their printing presses somewhere else."

Tom pushed open the wrought iron gate and they walked up a couple of steps leading to a tall paneled front door flanked by columns. Next to the door they saw a sign listing two professional offices.

"*The Stylist* is not the only business here, and there are a couple of private apartments too."

They made their way up to the first floor, through a set of glass doors which opened into a small reception area. The young woman sitting behind a desk wore a fashionable ensemble in light green and blue with a pale orange tie. She pushed back her reading glasses and welcomed them with a bright smile.

Evie introduced herself. "And this is Mr. Tom Winchester. I wonder if we might be able to speak with Margaret Thornbury."

"Do you have an appointment?"

"No, I'm afraid we don't."

"One moment please. I'll see if she's available." She picked up the telephone and spoke in a hushed tone. After a brief conversation, she disconnected the call and smiled. "Margaret Thornbury will see you in her apartment. It's on the fourth floor."

As they turned to leave, Evie looked beyond the glass partition behind the reception desk. She could see an open space with two desks and a number of cabinets. A young woman sat at her desk. Evie leaned forward but she didn't see anyone else.

Not exactly a large office environment, she thought.

They took the stairs to the fourth floor and found a lobby with two doors, each one marked with a name.

Tom pointed to the one at the front of the building and when he knocked, a butler answered.

They were shown through to a small drawing room where they were asked to wait.

"How does the Countess of Woodridge feel about being asked to wait?" Tom whispered.

"She knew we were coming. Maybe we interrupted an afternoon nap." In reality, she wondered if Margaret Thornbury wanted to gain the upper hand by making them wait.

Tom looked around the drawing room. "I thought everyone in the upper echelons of society lived in grand houses."

"This is grand enough on a small scale." Sumptuously decorated with beautiful antiques, she knew the drawing room would be one of many rooms in the apartment. One of her cousins in America had recently moved into an apartment in New York right opposite Central Park and she claimed it had been the best decision she'd ever made as the apartment offered plenty of space and easy access to all the entertainments in the city.

"Doesn't one of your cousins live in an apartment?"

"Yes, I was just thinking about that. Ruby recently moved into the Dakota. I believe she is trying to lead a bohemian lifestyle or land herself a bohemian husband. I can't remember which, and I'm not sure Toodles knows about it so I suggest steering clear of the subject."

"Is it likely to come up?" Tom laughed. "Don't worry. I just answered my own question. With Toodles, one never knows."

The door opened and Margaret Thornbury entered. "Lady Woodridge. To what do I owe the honor?" She raised an elegant hand. "Let me guess, this is about Jacinta McKay's death and I'm under suspicion."

CHAPTER 12

MARGARET THORNBURY'S lips curved into a knowing smile. "Lady Woodridge, you look baffled."

In other words, Evie thought, she was gaping. Evie closed her mouth and focused on providing a placid smile.

"Your name has been mentioned once or twice in relation to a couple of murder cases," Margaret said conversationally. "According to the rumor mills, you were at Madame Berger's shortly before Jacinta went there."

Elegantly tall with fine features and dramatic dark colored eyes, Margaret Thornbury walked across the room and before settling down on a chair opposite Tom and Evie, she reached for a silver case and helped herself to a cigarette.

Evie knew of at least one friend who smoked but never in public and rarely in company.

She watched with intrigue as Margaret Thornbury

adjusted the cigarette into an elegant holder, lit it and, tilting her chin up, blew out the smoke.

The owner of the magazine studied her for a moment. Settling back into her chair, she crossed her legs and studied her for a moment. "I would love to interview you, Lady Woodridge. The readers would find you fascinating." She turned to Tom and offered him a sultry smile. "And they would be equally interested in you, Mr. Winchester. Have you known Lady Woodridge long?"

"The Countess and I go back a long way."

Eager for some answers and before Margaret Thornbury could ask about the misleading photograph announcing her engagement, Evie said, "This is an interesting set up you have here, Mrs. Thornbury."

"I'm no longer married."

Evie guessed she was divorced. In her experience, if she had been a widow, the words would have carried the weight of her loss. Unless, of course, she hadn't cared much for her husband.

"Living here suits my hectic social life and it's quite handy to walk down to the office. Although, I do still tend to do most of my work here."

"I noticed you don't have many staff members working for you."

"No, there's no need to fill an office with people. Most articles are written by women who work from their homes. Jacinta McKay was the exception. She was one of my in-house writers and she also worked on the magazine layout. She will be missed."

Evie didn't detect any heartfelt sorrow over the loss.

Then again, not everyone wore their hearts on their sleeves. "Did she have family?"

Margaret Thornbury nodded. "Her father and mother live in the north where they own a mill." She studied her cigarette for a moment and then added, "Oh, and I believe they also have a coal mine. They were not exactly pleased with their daughter's choices."

"Her career choices?"

"Among other things. I shouldn't really say. In fact, I don't have all the details."

Evie didn't know how to broach the subject. The way Margaret Thornbury had expressed herself, it sounded as if Jacinta had made unorthodox personal choices.

"How well did you know her?" Tom asked.

Margaret Thornbury uncrossed her legs, shifted and crossed her legs again. "We had a working relationship."

"Did you get along with her?" Evie asked.

"As I said, we had a working relationship. She worked for me and she enjoyed the perks of her job. If she had any issues, she never expressed them to me."

Tom leaned forward. "Lady Woodridge recently *expressed* her disappointment over an article written by Jacinta McKay. She believes Jacinta might have been directed to write it."

"Hardly." Margaret Thornbury drew on her cigarette. "I trusted her judgement. She had free rein over what she wrote. I usually found out about the articles when the issues hit the streets."

Yet, Jacinta had suggested someone else had been responsible.

"Do you know if she'd had a falling out with anyone or if she'd had other critics?" Tom asked.

Evie glanced at him. If he suspected there might be other critics then, presumably, that would make her the first critic, perhaps even the primary critic...

Evie felt compelled to draw out her notebook and write a reminder to herself to tell Tom she had always been and would always be highly tolerant and accepting of opposing views, but she could never be entirely happy to be labeled a critic. It simply didn't sit well with her.

The magazine owner made a dismissive gesture with her hand and drew on her cigarette. "The world is full of critics. She probably received a dozen letters a week if not more." Turning to Evie, she added, "I'm surprised she read your letter. Jacinta normally disposed of them. Perhaps curiosity got the better of her. Did you by any chance threaten her?"

Evie's eyes widened. Gaping, she asked, "Me?"

Barely managing to hide his smile, Tom diverted the attention away from Evie. "Has the police spoken with you?"

"Yes, a rather stout looking man interrupted my afternoon yesterday."

"Detective Inspector O'Neill?"

"That's the one. No sense of decorum whatsoever. The police could at least dress in less drab tones." Margaret's eyes skated around Tom's face. "By the way, I like your tie. You might want to try wearing a more colorful vest. Perhaps yellow. A soft shade of Naples yellow. Yes, that should go nicely with light colored suits." She tipped her head to the side. "And pink vests with dark suits. You could revive the stripes that were in fashion during the Regency period."

"I'll keep that in mind." In the next breath, he asked, "Why do you think Jacinta McKay went to visit Madame Berger after she wrote such a critical article?"

Margaret Thornbury's eyebrows curved into a neat, expressive line. "I couldn't even begin to imagine. It doesn't actually make sense."

"Why do you say that?" Tom prodded.

"She had already written a piece on Madame Berger. Jacinta liked to stay on the move, so to speak. She made a point of keeping up to date with fashion. After all, that's what the magazine is about. Obviously, in her opinion, Madame Berger had reached her pinnacle of success and was now on the decline." She leaned forward and stubbed her cigarette out. "There are other designers in the building. Maybe Jacinta went to see one of them and then acted on impulse and went on to visit Madame Berger."

Distracted by some of the framed photographs on display, Evie missed part of the conversation. "So, you're suggesting she might have gone to see someone else."

"Yes, it's possible. You'd have to ask Alice. She manages the front desk downstairs. Sometimes, Jacinta told her where she planned on going." She gave them a brisk smile. "I could not have killed Jacinta. As it is, I have an issue coming out this week and no feature article."

Thanking her for her time, Evie stood up. "The newspaper didn't actually mention how she died and I don't believe anyone mentioned murder."

Margaret Thornbury gave an elegant shrug of her

shoulder. "An assumption on my part. When facts are not provided, one tends to assume."

Agreeing, Evie gave a small nod. As they left the elegant room, she cast her eyes around. Settling her attention on the photographs sitting on the mantlepiece, she saw one with Margaret and Jacinta on a rowing boat, a manor house in the distance.

So much for implying they'd only had a working relationship, she thought.

They made their way downstairs in silence. However, a few exchanged glances suggested they were both thinking about everything Margaret Thornbury had said and trying to read between the lines.

They found the receptionist, Alice, on the telephone, talking and scribbling a note.

As they waited for her to end the call, Tom nudged Evie and signaled to a stack of papers on Alice's desk.

Evie looked but she couldn't see what had caught his attention. She considered using her notebook to scribble a question, but then the receptionist finished her call and looked up.

Giving them a friendly smile, she asked, "How may I help you?"

"Margaret said you might be able to tell us if Jacinta McKay had mentioned anything about visiting someone on the day she died." Evie gave herself points for making it sound as though she and Margaret were the best of friends.

The receptionist looked around her desk, moved a

few stacks and then found a large appointment book. "Sometimes, she would tell me where she was going, but not always. Let me see... Oh, yes. Here it is. She'd set out to meet a couple of people and mentioned she might call on Adele Lawson."

"Adele Lawson?"

"She's a new designer who'd been trying to get Jacinta to write an article about her."

"Had Jacinta been happy about that?"

The receptionist wavered before saying, "Sometimes she gave young designers a mention. It all depended..."

"On what?"

Alice shrugged.

"Did it depend on what she could get?" Tom asked.

When Evie remembered Margaret Thornbury had mentioned Jacinta enjoying perks, she silently congratulated Tom on his perceptive question.

The receptionist grinned.

"Does Adele Lawson have an atelier in the same building as Madame Berger?" Evie asked.

The receptionist nodded and glanced at the telephone, almost as if willing it to ring, which it did.

Thanking her with a smile and a wave, they left. But not before taking another look at the receptionist's desk...

CHAPTER 13

Emerging from the building, Evie looked up and down the street, for no other reason other than to mirror Tom's habit.

Seeing them, Edmonds started the motor car.

They settled in the back seat in silence broken only by Edmonds who asked, "Where to, milady?"

Evie gave it some thought. She still needed to get the letter to the detective, but now she felt she needed to add some observations.

"The Savoy, Edmonds."

Tom checked his watch. "An early afternoon tea. Sounds good to me."

Evie had other ideas in mind but didn't mention them. "Yes, I suppose it is a good time for refreshments."

Evie shifted around until she succeeded in catching her reflection in the rearview mirror. She adjusted her hat, had another look and then set the hat back the way Caro liked it.

Out of the corner of her eye, she saw Tom gritting his teeth. "Your jaw muscles are working overtime."

"Nothing to do with Edmonds' driving," he assured her. "It's the pedestrians that are making me edgy. It's almost as if they're asking to be run over."

"They were here first, Tom."

"Yes, I can just picture you arguing with a motor car."

"Motor cars can be replaced. They should be mindful of where they're going. By the way, what were you trying to draw my attention to?"

He tipped his hat back. "The magazine on her desk. It was open and had a red circle around an advertisement. Under it, someone had written canceled. It had last week's date on it."

"I'm sure it's not unusual for advertisers to cancel. Then again, is your suspicious mind telling you they canceled because they were unhappy about something?"

He laughed. "I'm not usually the one with the suspicious mind."

"Yes, you're right. I believe I'm experiencing a lull. Or perhaps I'm subconsciously rebelling against Toodles' wish I take up the profession." So much for wanting her grandmother to be happy. "So, what else did you notice?"

"The advertisement appeared on a page with a Jacinta McKay article."

"Aha. Well, in that case, the information has to be included in my letter to the detective. He'll know whether or not it's worth pursuing."

Arriving at the Savoy, Evie said, "Edmonds, we shouldn't be longer than an hour."

"That's going to be one heck of a letter," Tom said.

"Since I'm only doing this once, I'd like to be thorough."

They walked up to the entrance and, to Evie's surprise, the doorman tipped his hat and greeted Tom by name.

"Mr. Winchester. It's a pleasure to see you here again."

"Harold. How's the missus?"

"Very well, sir. Thank you for asking."

Walking into the lobby, Evie's curiosity urged her to ask, "Mr. Winchester? Is this part of your mysterious past?"

As expected, he became evasive.

"That's it? You're not going to volunteer information?" Evie nudged him and steered him away from the restaurant.

Tom's eyebrows lifted. "The American Bar? Isn't it a little early for drinking?"

"It'll be quieter here. I need to focus."

As soon as they sat at a small corner table, Evie dug inside her handbag and drew out the letter she had written to the detective. "I need to include some pertinent facts. I just can't decide what they will be."

A waiter approached the table to take their orders.

Tom cleared his throat and checked his watch again. "A coffee, please."

Evie found her small fountain pen and set it down on the table. "I'll have a Hanky-Panky, please."

The waiter nodded and walked off.

"Cocktails in the afternoon?"

"You disapprove? Is that why you ordered coffee?"

Tom drummed his fingers on the table. "I assumed we were here to work. Clearly, that was a mistake."

"It would be sacrilegious to sit at the Savoy's American Bar and not drink a cocktail. Do you want the waiter to get into trouble?" She spread the letter out and skimmed through it. "Now, what do you think I can add to this?"

"I would have liked to know more about Jacinta's parents objecting to her choices," Tom said.

Evie agreed. "I think we were meant to guess what their objections might be." She leaned in and whispered, "She might have been having an affair." Evie looked down at the letter and wondered if Jacinta might have had an affair with a woman. That would certainly raise a few eyebrows. She imagined Jacinta's parents would not have been pleased about it. Although, she couldn't think what any of that would have to do with her death. Unless...

What if the person she'd been having an affair with killed her?

Looking up, she saw Tom waving at someone at the bar.

A woman approached carrying Evie's cocktail and Tom's coffee.

Tom gave her a bright smile. "Ada Coleman! Still mixing drinks?" He turned to Evie and made the introduction. "This is the Countess of Woodridge."

The pretty blonde looked to be in her forties. She gave Evie an easy smile. "I assume the coffee is for you, Mr. Winchester, and the cocktail for Lady Woodridge." She winked at him. "I made you an Irish without the cream."

"Bless your heart, Coley." Tom took a sip of his coffee and smiled. "You're the bee's knees." He turned to Evie. "You know she created the Hanky-Panky."

"How marvelous."

"Tell Lady Woodridge the story," Tom encouraged.

Ada Coleman smiled. "Charles Hawtrey, the English actor, came in one day and asked for something with a bit of punch in it. I spent hours experimenting until I finally got it. He took one sip and, draining the glass, said it was a real hanky-panky."

"Do you think you could come up with a cocktail for Lady Woodridge? You could call it the Birdie. Something yellow, I think."

The bartender gave it some thought. "I could do one with Galliano liqueur. It's yellow."

"Perfect."

Nodding, she said, "I'll get to work on it straightaway." The bartender walked off with a light spring in her step.

Looking at her cocktail, Evie said, "There's no getting out of it now. You have to tell me how you came to be on such friendly terms with the staff."

He took his time drinking his coffee and when he finished, he said, "It was during the war. Whenever we took leave, we stayed at the Savoy."

"We? You and who else?"

"Viscount Strathmore."

"Viscount Strathmore?" Evie prompted. She knew most returned soldiers preferred to avoid the subject but she hadn't asked for actual details about the war.

"When he insisted on a commission and going to the front lines, his family agreed on the condition he took me along. He was the only heir and my job was to make sure he came back in one piece."

That had been the cover story he'd given when they'd attended the Duke of Hetherington's house party. Evie reminded him about it. "Are you saying that wasn't a made-up story?"

Instead of answering, he pointed at the letter. "Have you decided if you'll add anything else?"

Evie took a moment to savor her drink. "What did Margaret Thornbury mean when she said she'd had a working relationship with Jacinta? I think she tried to be diplomatic. Do you think she merely tolerated Jacinta?"

"You have a multitude of people working for you. With a few exceptions, I'd say you have working relationships with them. You are cordial, everyone respects each other and harmony prevails."

"Who are the exceptions?" she asked.

"Caro and Edgar. They are on a more familiar footing with you."

As for Tom Winchester, Evie thought...

Strictly speaking, she did not employ him. Toodles did. Or did she? What sort of arrangement had her granny made with Tom?

"I get the feeling Margaret Thornbury was less than friendly with Jacinta. I might even go so far as to suggest she might have been aloof. I noticed a hint of dismissiveness when she mentioned Jacinta's parents own a mill up north. As if that made them less distinguished. Then again..."

"What?"

"I'm not sure what to make of it, but I saw a photograph of Margaret and Jacinta together. They looked quite friendly."

"Some people have no trouble appearing to be on the best of terms."

Evie took another drink and added, "I might mention something about the choices Jacinta presumably made. That could lead the detective to a significant person in Jacinta's life who might know something about possible enemies. Also, Jacinta might have confided in someone. I assume the police will eventually find her death suspicious, warranting further investigation into it. Yes, indeed. A lover or someone close to her could provide some insight." She finished her drink and turned her attention to making a few additions to her letter.

"Have you decided how you'll deliver the letter?" Tom asked.

"I might end up asking you to deliver it. The detective didn't warn you to steer clear of the investigation and I have a feeling he would be more tolerant with you." Leaning forward, she checked Tom's watch. "Let's see if we can find Adele Lawson. I'd be interested to know if she got on well with Jacinta. In any case, she might have some worthwhile information I could add." Evie folded the letter and returned it to the envelope. "Shall we go?"

"Coley's coming and she's bringing a cocktail. We wouldn't want to hurt her feelings."

The bartender set down a martini glass in front of Evie. "The Birdie."

Without hesitating, Evie lifted the glass. "To the Birdie." Taking a sip, her eyes brightened. "This is marvelous." She took another sip. "Suddenly, I feel like jumping in a roadster and whizzing up Oxford Street. Better still, along The Mall, and all the way up to the palace gates."

"And," Tom said, "I suddenly see the benefit of Edmonds driving us around."

CHAPTER 14

EVIE HUMMED ALL the way back to Madame Berger's. "Remind me again why we're going to visit Adele Lawson."

"If we are to believe Margaret Thornbury's receptionist, we think Jacinta went to see her before she went to see Madame Berger. I believe that is your official line. The unofficial one being that you are determined to defy the detective and uncover something before he does."

Evie ignored the taunt. "Maybe something Adele Lawson said prompted Jacinta to confront Madame Berger. I can't think of any reason why she would want to see her again after writing that dreadful article." Evie shook her head and grumbled under her breath.

Once a paragon of fashion, now outdated...

"It didn't turn out into much of a confrontation when she dropped dead before she could say anything," Tom said.

"You seem to forget we do not trust Madame

Berger. Jacinta went to see her for a reason. She didn't just drop dead on the spot. Surely, she must have suffered some ill effects. Assuming she felt ill, why would she make the effort to see Madame Berger?"

"Perhaps she wanted to ask for forgiveness. Or... she might have wanted to confess to something. If that's the case, we'll never know what she wanted to say because Madame Berger will not share the information. What about Lucy, her young receptionist? Do you trust her?"

"She might have been coerced into lying." Glancing out the window, she watched the world going about its business. "Someone must know something about Jacinta's intentions." She gave a firm nod. If Adele Lawson had been the last person to speak with Jacinta, then she must know something about Jacinta's state of mind. "We think Madame Berger lied and she must obviously have a very good reason. Although, what that might be, we have no idea."

"Is that a royal we?" Tom asked.

"Pardon?"

"You said *we* think she lied."

"Oh... No, it's a you and I." Evie grinned. "We're engaged, remember?"

Tom looked astonished by the news. "And engaged people refer to themselves in the plural?"

"All the time. I think it's because it saves time. Easier to say *we* instead of so and so and I. In our case, Tom and I." Evie gasped.

"What?"

"That last drink went straight to my head. When we saw Jacinta coming out of the building, she must have just been to see Adele Lawson. After our brief confrontation, I assume she returned to the office. At which point, she read the letter and that's when she returned. Why have I been thinking she went to see someone else before confronting Madame Berger? There's no reason for it. So, it must be the drink."

"You were thinking it before you had a drink."

Evie looked up and sighed. "The drinks have nothing to do with it. I just need to stop asking questions. Without any answers, I'm getting all muddled up. And, truth be known, I am torn. On the one hand, the matter is being dealt with by the police, so we shouldn't become involved. However, on the other hand, who knows what we might find out?" She remembered Martin Gate saying he didn't care to be told what to do. Did she feel the same way? Did she resent the detective for singling her out and asking her not to meddle? "No," she whispered.

"No?"

"I was just thinking the police have a job to do and I shouldn't really question their tactics even when they have an impact on me."

"Nonsense. You've been helpful in the past. I say they are wrong to try to sanction you." He glanced at her. "Yes? No?"

"Yes, you're right. Their focus should be on solving the crime any way they can." Evie straightened. "Jacinta visited the building twice." She repeated the statement several times so the fact would sink in.

"Are you trying to wring out the truth from those few words?"

"I suppose we'll know soon enough if Jacinta visited Adele Lawson early in the day or closer to midday. I should have drawn up some sort of timeline." Grumbling, she added, "In reality, I should decide if I want to help. And, if I do, I should throw myself into the task. Having said that, I honestly don't wish to get the detective into any trouble with his superior."

Hiding his smile by looking away, Tom said, "I'm sure Detective O'Neill would be only too happy to liaise with you in secret."

When Edmonds brought the motor car to a stop, Tom jumped out and held the door open for her.

Evie tried to catch his attention by leaning and waving. "A hand, please?"

Tom peered inside. "Are you stuck?"

Evie giggled. "I think The Birdie really did go to my head or my legs. I can't tell..."

Tom straightened, looked up and down the street, and then reached in. "Am I going to have to haul you out and lug you up the stairs?"

Evie stepped out of the car. Reaching for her hat, she forgot she held her handbag. In the next breath, she lost her balance and toppled forward. Tom caught her and, laughing, he swept her off her feet and carried her across the sidewalk. Reaching the first step leading up to the building, he set her down.

"I don't know what your friend put in that drink but it has quite a punch to it. Am I slurring my words?"

"Not yet."

Straightening, Evie asked, "What was that all about?"

"What?"

"You looked around before you helped me."

"Oh, that was just a precautionary measure. We

wouldn't want you to wake up to a photograph of you being dragged out of a motor car. That wouldn't be very Countess-like."

"I don't know why I asked. I already know you take your bodyguard duties seriously. By the way, since you profess to be as rich as Croesus, who keeps an eye on you? What if someone tried to kidnap you and held you for ransom? And, if you're really wealthy, what are you doing parading around as my bodyguard? Never mind. I just heard myself. I'm rambling. Although, I am still curious."

"Even wealthy people need something to do. Remember, I have humble beginnings."

"Just how rich do you pretend to be?"

"Not as rich as you and not as rich as... Rockefeller. I believe his net worth in 1913 was $900 million."

Evie whistled. "I don't think I have that many millions."

"But you do have quite a few and that begs the question. What are you doing living in the backwoods of a foreign country when you could be living the high life in the Riviera?"

"I don't live in the backwoods. In any case, I happen to like where I live. It's peaceful and charming."

Climbing the steps to the front door of the building, Evie gave her sleeves a tug and drew in a deep breath.

"Ready?" Tom asked.

"I'm not sure. What if... Oh, I do hope this pays off."

Tom laughed.

"What's so funny?"

"I thought you might be worried about falling on

your face. Rest assured, I'll be happy to prop you up so you don't slide off a chair."

"Yes, do stick close to me. I guess there's a lesson to learn from this. Never mix the Hanky-Panky with The Birdie."

They found Adele Lawson's salon on the second floor. "If we're to believe Margaret Thornbury's receptionist, Jacinta came here. Then, something happened to her... Within moments after leaving Adele Lawson's salon, she fell ill and, for some reason, she made her way up to Madame Berger's... Why did she do that?"

When a young woman answered the door, they introduced themselves. To Evie's surprise, Adele Lawson recognized Evie.

"I think everyone has seen the photograph, my lady. I haven't read an announcement. Are congratulations really in order?" Adele asked.

Evie smiled but before she could say anything, Tom spoke up. "Yes. That's why we're here. Lady Woodridge wishes to have a new dress designed for the wedding."

Adele Lawson looked surprised. "Really?"

"Oh, yes. She is quite determined."

While still looking doubtful, Adele Lawson took a step back and showed them through to a large room set up as a showroom with a couple of chairs flanking a fireplace.

"You'll have to excuse me if I look surprised. I was under the impression you were Madame Berger's exclusive client."

"Oh... Yes, well..." Evie bought herself some thinking time by removing her gloves. "I feel like a change and I'd like to support a young designer."

"That's very gracious of you, my lady."

"Have you found others equally supportive?" Evie asked. "I imagine you would benefit greatly by having an article written about your designs."

"Yes, any publicity would be good. Do you have any ideas about what sort of dress you would like?"

Evie exchanged a look with Tom and wondered if he shared the feeling Adele had tried to change the subject. "I was rather hoping you might be able to inspire me."

"Yes, of course. Perhaps we could start by looking at my drawings. I'll only be a moment." Adele Lawson excused herself and went through to an adjoining room.

Evie mouthed, "Wedding dress?"

Tom shrugged. "I had to say something to justify our visit."

"At this rate, Mr. Winchester, I might need you to provide an engagement ring."

"That could be arranged. Do you favor any particular stone?"

Evie looked down at her left hand. A while back, she'd decided that phase of her life had come to an end so she had forced herself to remove her rings. She had never considered wearing another man's rings.

She leaned back on her chair and tried to come up with a humorous remark. She was about to say the first thing that came to her when she heard a whizzing... whistling sound.

"Did you hear that?"

Tom looked around and pointed to the fireplace. "I think it's coming from there."

They both leaned down.

Evie thought she heard a voice. Or rather, a conversational murmur and then she made out Madame Berger's voice. She'd dropped her accent!

"Can you make out what she's saying?"

Tom pressed a finger to his other ear. After a moment, he shook his head.

They were so immersed in their efforts to listen to the sounds coming from the chimney, they didn't hear Adele Lawson returning.

When she set a large folder down on a table, they were both startled.

"Is something wrong?" Adele Lawson asked.

"We thought we heard voices," Tom said.

Adele glanced at the fireplace. "Sound travels in this building." Sitting down opposite them, she searched through the folder. When she found what she wanted, she looked at Evie. "Do you have any color preferences?"

"Color?" Evie's thoughts were still distracted by the murmurs wafting down from the floors above.

"The Countess prefers green but that wouldn't do for a wedding gown. I think the palest shade of gold would be splendid."

Evie winced. "That sounds like *beige*."

"Then that's settled. Beige it is," Tom said. "The Countess loves beige."

Adele Lawson looked down at her collection of drawings. After a moment, she sat back. "You'll have to excuse my bluntness, but I get the feeling you are not really here because you want me to design your wedding dress."

"As a matter of fact, Mr. Winchester and I were curious to know why Jacinta McKay came to visit you and if she actually mentioned going to see Madame Berger. Of course, I am also interested in a dress."

"A wedding dress," Tom said.

They both looked at each other, their gazes holding for a moment, their eyes not even blinking.

"A wedding dress," Adele echoed.

Without breaking eye contact, they nodded. Then, as if by mutual agreement, they both turned their attention back to the young designer.

Evie spoke first, "We understand Jacinta came to see you. Was she going to write an article about you?"

"Yes, but..." Adele shook her head. "Never mind. So, have you set the date?"

"Did she set conditions?" Tom asked.

Adele looked down at her hands. "I've heard about such things happening so I knew what to expect. It's actually a fair exchange. She would have walked around in one of my designs and I would have received the publicity."

"Is that all she wanted?" Evie asked.

Adele did not hesitate to say, "Yes."

"Did she visit you later in the day?"

She responded with a small nod.

"What time?"

"Just before midday."

"It must have been a brief visit," Tom said.

Adele nodded. "She didn't stay long."

Tom and Evie exchanged a look of surprise.

Leaning forward, Tom asked, "How did she look?"

"Distracted. She sat down. Jumped to her feet. Then she sat down again. Finally, she left."

"Did you happen to hear anything after that?" Evie

signaled toward the fireplace. "We understand the incident took place close to midday."

"I'm not sure. I think I might have been out."

And that, Evie thought, didn't really answer her question.

"Has the police spoken with you?"

"I believe they spoke with all the tenants in the building." Adele looked down at her book of designs. "Did you want a long or short veil? Lace or satin?"

CHAPTER 15

"Will you be adding our conversation with Adele Lawson to your letter?" Tom asked even before they reached the stairs.

"It might be worth mentioning how sound travels through the chimney." Evie stopped and looked up. "I wonder if we should speak with Louisa Barclay?" She didn't wait for a response from Tom. "No. This letter needs to go right now. Except, I still haven't decided how we should deliver it." She stopped and smiled. "Oh, I know." Brightening, Evie slipped her arm through Tom's and led him down the stairs. "Time to pay Mrs. Lotte Mannering a visit."

They found Edmonds leaning against the motor car. When he saw them, he promptly held the door open for them. Giving him the address to Lotte Mannering's office, Evie settled back and smiled. Why hadn't she thought of it before?

"Toodles is not going to like this," Tom warned.

"When you promised you'd visit Lotte Mannering, I think she assumed she would be going along."

"We'll cross that bridge when we come to it. Or, rather, we should do our best to avoid it altogether. She mustn't find out. Besides, it's going to be a quick visit to organize the delivery of this letter and then we'll return to the house and organize ourselves for dinner."

"I hope you realize we don't have any books with us."

"Books?"

"Our alibi for slipping out without letting them know," Tom reminded her.

"We'll figure something out or we could say we looked but didn't find anything appropriate. After all, Seth already has so many books. At some point, it was bound to become difficult to find anything that would interest him."

"You seem to have it all covered now. I take it the cocktails have worked themselves out of your system."

"Not quite. When it comes to offering my grandmother explanations, I've always been able to think on my feet. It's a survival skill. And, strictly speaking, everything I've said is based on truth. Seth will have to hurry up and start expanding his interests."

Edmonds stopped in front of a building that stood out because of its ordinariness. It didn't have any columns, ornaments or balconies. Even the brass door knocker had a simple design. Not that they needed it since the front door stood ajar.

"We shouldn't be too long, Edmonds." Turning to look out of the window, Evie nudged Tom. "Oh, look. There's a bookstore next door. Fate is on our side." At least, Evie thought, something seemed to be working in their favor. With everyone so obviously lying through their teeth, she pitied the detective. How on earth would he ever find the culprit?

There were several business names listed at the door. Lotte Mannering had an office on the first floor.

They walked in and were greeted by an elderly lady with graying hair. She stood in front of a large desk humming under her breath as she sifted through a stack of files.

"Good afternoon." Tom removed his hat. "We would like to speak with Mrs. Lotte Mannering, please."

The woman set the file aside and pushed back her glasses.

Evie nudged Tom with her elbow.

"What?" he mouthed.

"Mrs. Mannering is currently on a case." The woman sniffed and pushed her glasses back again.

Evie gave her a warm smile. "Very well, then... I'm sorry, I didn't catch your name."

"Gloria."

"Gloria, perhaps you can help us. We have a letter we would like Lotte Mannering to deliver to Detective O'Neill."

"Is she acquainted with him?" The elderly receptionist's tone sounded slightly annoyed and impatient.

"She knows of him and you can drop the act, Lotte."

The woman blinked. "Pardon?"

"I know it's you."

Removing her glasses, the receptionist wiped them with a handkerchief and put them back on. "I'm afraid you have made a mistake, my lady."

"Is that so? I don't remember Tom introducing me as Lady Woodridge. So how did you know to address me as my lady?"

"I read the newspapers, *my lady*."

Tom leaned in for a closer look. "Lotte? Is that really you?"

The woman pressed her lips together until the edges turned white. Finally, she huffed out a breath. "Oh, very well. Yes, it is me. How on earth could you tell?"

"The eyes," Evie revealed.

Lotte held her gaze for a moment and then reached inside a drawer. Holding a compact mirror in front of her, she muttered, "The color of my eyes or the shape?"

"The shape. They're close together."

"Well, there's nothing I can do about that." Lotte turned to Tom. "Yet, you didn't recognize me."

"I don't seem to be as observant as the Countess. I admit, once I saw your gray hair, I formed assumptions."

Lotte put away the mirror and crossed her arms. "I suppose I could settle for fooling one of you."

"Are you on a case?" Evie asked.

"No, I've been trying out a new disguise."

"You look... rather curvy. If not for the eyes, you would have fooled me."

Lotte grinned. "Padding. You'd be surprised how much a person can change with a few extra pounds. Even the way I walk changes. No one would recognize me in this disguise. Well, no one other than you." She signaled toward her office. "Go on through, I'll join you in a moment."

Tom and Evie walked into a small office with

windows facing the street. There were several filing cabinets pushed up against one wall and a large desk in the middle of the room. As she sat down, Evie wobbled slightly on the chair that had seen better days.

Glancing around, Evie said, "I'm almost sorry I mentioned recognizing her. It seemed to upset her."

"Do you blame her? She clearly put a lot of effort into transforming herself."

Evie looked over her shoulder and studied the collection of clothes piled up on a table at the opposite end of the room. "I must say, if she had dressed up as an elderly lady when we first met her, I might not have suspected her of being a lady detective. Like you, I would have been fooled by the gray hair."

They heard her heavy footsteps as she moved around the outer office. A moment later, she approached the office only to stop at the door when someone entered.

"Is she not back yet?"

Evie looked at Tom and mouthed, "Henrietta?"

He nodded.

"It's been an hour. You said she would return in an hour."

Evie mouthed again, "Toodles?"

They both turned and leaned back to try to catch a glimpse of them.

Lotte Mannering scoffed. "She will be back when she is back."

"I could not possibly drink another cup of tea."

This time, they heard Sara speak.

Clearly, they had not seen past Lotte's disguise.

"We will wait here." Henrietta sounded quite determined. "We have some important business to discuss with her. It is imperative that we speak with her today. Is there any way for you to contact her? Couldn't you send someone out with a message for her?"

"I'm afraid not, my lady. She could be anywhere."

Evie pressed her hand to her mouth. Lotte Mannering had spent Christmas with them and, during that time, she had shared many of her lady detective stories, most of them quite incredible and daring. How could they not recognize her?

Tom leaned in and whispered, "I'm sure I would eventually have recognized her."

"Toodles isn't saying much," Evie whispered back. "I can picture her studying Lotte and wondering where she'd seen her before."

"We shall wait in her office," Henrietta declared.

"I'm afraid that is not possible."

Lotte tried to block the way, but the dowagers and Toodles ignored her and piled right in. When they saw Evie and Tom, they all came to an abrupt stop and gasped.

Henrietta employed her haughtiest tone to say, "Evangeline, I am speechless. You went behind our backs."

"We might say the same about you," Evie replied. "What are you all doing here?"

Lotte Mannering, still playing the role of Gloria, the elderly receptionist, pushed past them and went to stand behind the desk. "This is highly irregular. Mrs. Mannering has confidential information stored in here. She is not going to be pleased. I should contact the constabulary and have you all hauled out of here."

Evie thought Lotte might be pushing her luck.

As Henrietta declared, "I would like to see you try," Tom stood up and gave up his chair.

"Some tea would be much appreciated. At least, for me." Henrietta said. "Oh, and more chairs, please." Sniffing the air, she cast her eye around the office. "A blackboard. Do you think Lotte Mannering has taken up the teaching profession?"

"I believe she is committed to her current occupation," Evie suggested. "The blackboard might be used to work out her cases."

"I see. How ingenious. And did you have a fruitful afternoon? I don't see you carrying any books so I suspect that might have been a ruse."

Evie saw no point in avoiding the subject since they would get the information out of her one way or another. "I couldn't justify appearing at Margaret Thornbury's doorstep with an entourage in tow. After speaking with the magazine owner and Adele Lawson, a young designer, Tom and I reached the conclusion they are both lying. Since the detective has spoken to both women, I assume he has reached the same conclusion." She looked up and tried to think if she had left anything out. "What brought you here?"

Henrietta exchanged a look with the others that suggested she might have been trying to seek their support.

Evie realized she really had set something into motion by writing that letter to Jacinta McKay. Henrietta expected to see some action and, so far, Evie had failed to provide it.

"You'd promised we would visit Lotte Mannering.

Yet you came here without us. And don't get me started on your determination to leave everything to the police."

"You seem to have a problem with that, Henrietta."

"Yes, of course, I do. The newspapers are not reporting on the incident. The police are being cagey. As a citizen, I believe I have the right to answers. Also, I side with your grandmother. Your skills are going to waste. If you put your mind to it, you would have this case wrapped up in no time."

"And you came here because…"

"We thought we should have a word with Lotte Mannering. We believe she might be able to talk you into joining her in this enterprise. She could be your mentor."

"Really?"

"Oh, very well. We wish to engage her services. Since the police refuses to keep us informed, we will do some digging ourselves. Or, rather, we will ask Lotte Mannering to do it for us."

Just then, Lotte returned with a couple of chairs for Sara and Toodles and grumbled, "There is no tea and… Mrs. Mannering won't like this one bit."

"If she is on a case, she will have to abandon it because we have some pressing matters which need to be attended to with the greatest urgency." Henrietta gave a firm nod. "Lady Woodridge has discovered everyone she spoke with has lied and we think the detective needs to look at Jacinta's personal life."

"Jacinta?" Lotte asked.

"Good heavens, woman. Don't you read the newspapers?" Henrietta exclaimed.

Evie leaned in. "The name hasn't been reported, Henrietta. No one else knows the identity of the person who died at the fashion house."

"Oh... Yes, of course. My apologies. Jacinta McKay died by nefarious means. At least, we think she did. Anyhow, we want Lotte Mannering to find out all she can about her private life. Where she lived and anything else she can uncover." Henrietta nudged her head toward the blackboard. "You should write this down."

Looking over her shoulder, Evie saw Toodles standing by the table with the pile of clothes.

"Are these the clothes Lotte Mannering uses to disguise herself?" Toodles picked up a gentleman's suit and held it up against her.

Before Lotte could answer, Henrietta gestured to the blackboard and spoke up, "You may start by listing the names of everyone who might have wanted Jacinta McKay dead." She ran through the names and looked at Evie for confirmation. "Have I left anyone or anything out?" Henrietta prompted Evie with a slight lift of her eyebrow.

Surprised, Evie shook her head. Henrietta rarely put on a display of determination. When she did, she could be quite tenacious.

Looking away, Evie caught Lotte Mannering's raised eyebrow.

Shifting in her chair, Evie glanced at Tom just as he raised his eyebrow.

It seemed everyone had decided to express themselves in silence.

Sighing, Evie gave them a few more details about their visit to Adele Lawson's studio. "We think she might have heard something. Sound travels through the chimney and we haven't actually spoken with Louisa Barclay. I assume she will merely confirm everything Madame Berger and Lucy said."

"So Adele Lawson could be a key witness," Henrietta mused. "Why would she withhold information?"

Evie held up the letter. "I'm sure the detective will get to the bottom of it all." She made a move to get up but Henrietta signaled for her to sit down again.

"We haven't finished yet."

"What else do you wish to do, Henrietta?"

"While we wait for Lotte Mannering, we could try some of these costumes on," Toodles suggested.

Lotte growled. "Mrs. Mannering would not like that."

Toodles shrugged. "She's not here to object."

Evie turned and looked at Sara who gave her a brisk smile. "In case you're wondering why I'm here, I didn't have anything else on this afternoon."

Lotte, still pretending to be Gloria, stepped back from the blackboard. "Anything else, my lady?"

Henrietta tapped her chin in thought. "Is it possible to write the names in different colors?"

Evie gave her an incredulous look. "You want to color coordinate the suspects?"

"I believe it would help."

"Does this moustache suit me?" Toodles asked.

Everyone turned and saw Toodles wearing a man's jacket and hat and she had somehow managed to press a fake moustache which hung askew under her nose.

"Well? Isn't anyone going to say something?" Toodles demanded.

Sara spoke up, saying, "You will probably need a full beard to hide the fact you are a woman."

"I'm inclined to agree."

One by one, everyone turned toward the door where the detective stood.

CHAPTER 16

Evie surged to her feet. "Detective O'Neill."

"My lady. Are you about to offer an explanation?"

Henrietta scoffed at the idea. "I do believe we are at complete liberty to come and go as we please. We are not plotting an uprising, detective."

The detective glanced at the blackboard. "But you are plotting something, my lady."

"I see you are captivated by our progress. We have been quite industrious. Is there anything on that blackboard you might find of interest, detective?"

"Voices from the chimney?" The detective looked straight at Evie.

"It's all right here in this letter, detective." Belatedly, Evie remembered she hadn't included any information about her chat with Adele Lawson so she filled him in. "I am being presumptuous in thinking you might not have established some of the facts included here, but I meant well." Having accomplished her task, Evie made her way to the door only to be stopped by Henrietta's protest.

"I refuse to leave without first getting some answers from the detective."

Evie tried to employ reason. "Henrietta, you know very well the detective is under strict orders."

"He owes us," Henrietta insisted. "The man has been a guest at your home. In the past, he has reaped the rewards of your intuitive nature. Do I need to say more?"

Tom wove his way to the door and joined Evie there.

"Not you too," Henrietta complained. "What about Lotte Mannering? Didn't you wish to speak with her? You didn't come all this way to simply hand her an envelope." Henrietta then turned on the detective, her eyes steeling with fierce determination. "And what brings you here, detective? Are you going to engage the lady detective's services? Clearly, you need assistance and since you cannot seek Lady Woodridge's help, you have to look elsewhere for an equally intuitive mind."

Evie leaned in and whispered to Tom, "I could really do with another Birdie."

"As a matter of fact, my lady, I am here at Lotte Mannering's behest. She telephoned me a short while ago to say you were all here."

Henrietta brightened. "Oh, you have come to your senses and have decided to join our side."

"Wait a minute," Toodles said, "how did she know we were here?"

The detective looked perplexed.

Lotte removed her wig and took her place behind

her desk. Opening the top drawer, she produced a bottle of whisky.

Henrietta spluttered, "You deceived us."

Lotte poured herself a generous amount of whisky and drank the lot in one gulp. "There I was enjoying a quiet afternoon..." She poured herself another glass. Holding up the bottle, she offered everyone a drink.

When they all declined, she set the bottle down on her desk and sat back to drink her second glass of whisky. "Never mind."

Henrietta looked up at Evie and Tom. "You might as well make yourselves comfortable."

Lotte leaned forward and eyeballed Henrietta. "Lady Woodridge has completed her task by personally delivering the letter to the detective. What more could you possibly want?"

"The truth, of course. The detective needs to tell us how Jacinta McKay died. Surely, the results must be back by now. We promise to keep the news to ourselves."

The detective turned and looked at the blackboard. "Strychnine."

Without saying anything, Evie sat down again.

"Miss Jacinta McKay had a cocaine addiction," the detective added.

"Are you suggesting she inhaled the poison?" Henrietta asked.

Continuing to study the blackboard, he gave a pensive nod.

Henrietta looked thoroughly confounded by the idea. "Could she not tell the difference between one substance and the other?"

Instead of answering, the detective turned to Evie. "Did you speak with Louisa Barclay?"

"No, Tom and I ran out of time. I really wanted to get the letter to you."

He picked up the piece of chalk and underlined her name on the blackboard. "We suspect she might have contacted the newspaper. Sometimes, they offer money in exchange for an alert to any newsworthy items."

He suspected but he couldn't be sure?

"Does that mean she had money worries?" Toodles asked. "Or did she simply take advantage of the situation?"

"She recently received an inheritance from her aunt and before that, her family had been quite supportive. In any case, her business has been doing well. She has an established clientele, albeit a small one," he explained.

Yet, he suspected she had contacted the newspaper for a price. What would compel a person to do that? Greed or mischief?

Henrietta looked confused. "So, if she didn't do it for the money, then what other reason do you think she had for contacting the newspaper?"

Evie wondered why the detective had chosen to share that piece of information with them when he couldn't even be sure Louisa Barclay had made the telephone call.

"It's possible she wished to draw attention to Madame Berger's salon as a way of harming her business," he said. "Society ladies would distance themselves—"

"Nonsense." Henrietta laughed. "It didn't keep us away."

"The detective might be right. Money could be behind the death," Toodles shrugged. "All these designers must be in serious competition. They could be trying to create more business for themselves by getting rid of one designer. We can't forget this all started with an article which discredited Madame Berger's creative abilities."

Still looking confused, Henrietta asked, "Is that a certainty? I thought all this started with Evangeline's letter of complaint."

Lotte had just been taking a drink. When it ended up going down the wrong way, she coughed until her face turned bright red.

"Good heavens," Henrietta exclaimed. "You might want to put some ice or water in your whisky instead of drinking it straight."

"Money is definitely involved," the detective mused.

Evie thought about perks. What if Jacinta had been asking for much more than just a few dresses? If she had become greedy, it could have given someone motive for murder.

"Are you able to determine if Jacinta suddenly experienced a flow of extra money?" Evie asked.

He nodded. "A considerable amount. We're trying to establish where it came from."

If it didn't come from an inheritance then, it might have been gained through suspicious means, Evie reasoned.

Henrietta smiled at the detective. "Wouldn't it be a simple matter of investigating people's banking details?"

"One would think so," he said. "But it's not always so simple. A cash deposit will be impossible to trace."

Had Jacinta extorted money for favorable reviews? When she put the question to the others, they all looked at the detective for an answer.

"We are pursuing that theory," he offered.

"Since Madame Berger received an unflattering review," Evie said, "it would stand to reason she had refused to pay up."

Henrietta lifted her chin and gave a firm nod. "Detective, assuming your theory is correct, if you work on a process of elimination, you should start with Madame Berger." She tapped her finger on the armrest to emphasize her point. "Make her admit to refusing to pay Jacinta McKay."

The detective brushed a hand over his chin. "And how should I then proceed, my lady?"

Henrietta blinked several times and then turned to Evie, lowering her voice to say, "The detective is in desperate need of assistance. You must help him, Evangeline." She turned back to the detective and shrugged. "I'm afraid I am all out of ideas at the moment but if anything comes up, I'll be sure to tell you about it."

Sara cleared her throat and looked around from one person to the other. "Are we now saying Jacinta had been extorting money?"

"We're not sure," Evie said.

"Oh, I see. We are still hypothesizing."

Detective O'Neill slipped the letter into the pocket of his coat and made a move to leave.

Henrietta put her hand up. "I have another question for the detective. I believe Evangeline is quite eager to find out who identified her as the person involved in a public altercation with Jacinta. You must understand, detective, her reputation is at stake here. We know Evangeline would never become involved in a public brawl, but others might be only too happy to think her capable of such behavior and we simply cannot have people saying the Countess of Woodridge is behaving like a fishmonger's wife."

"Henrietta," Evie's voice filled with caution. "The detective is not at liberty to divulge any information. He has probably already said too much."

"And yet I still believe you have the right to know the name of your accuser. There must be a way to find out the person's identity."

Hiding his smile, the detective said, "The information came to us anonymously."

Henrietta didn't look convinced. "But you said it had been a witness statement."

Evie felt for the detective. He looked utterly defeated. Not necessarily by Henrietta's remarks, but rather by something else. While his lips lifted into a smile, his eyes showed a world of weariness.

"My apologies. I had been directed to employ the tactic."

"You lied to us?" Henrietta could not have looked more incensed. "It's that Superintendent's doing."

Evie shifted to the edge of her chair. "I think even detectives working a case need to get dinner and a good night's rest."

"But we haven't discussed what we are going to do next," Henrietta complained.

As Evie leaned over to look at Tom's watch, she grabbed hold of a thought. Frowning, she stood up.

"This anonymous person who says she witnessed an altercation... What did she have to gain by it?"

"Precisely," Henrietta declared. "We must know her identity. How else are we going to give her a thorough dressing-down? Heavens, what if this was a deliberate attempt to implicate the Countess of Woodridge? Think about it. Evangeline wrote the letter of complaint, then she is seen arguing with the deceased..."

Lotte Mannering swiveled on her chair. "Am I on the case or not?"

CHAPTER 17

Evie couldn't stop laughing at Henrietta's outrage.

Hire Lotte Mannering?

Despite her earlier enthusiasm for the lady detective, the dowager had changed her mind and had expressed her dissatisfaction with Lotte Mannering, saying she had shown a lack of loyalty when she'd contacted the detective.

"And then what happened?" Caro asked as Evie dressed for dinner.

"Lotte Mannering had to explain her actions. It took some doing to pacify the dowager."

Caro hummed under her breath. "Her ladyship had a right to be annoyed with the lady detective."

"Anyhow, Lotte knows I have contributed to the detective's investigations and wanted to avoid treading on his toes so she thought it would be best to get us all together in the one room."

"Did it work?"

"I think it's too early to tell. I get the feeling the

detective wishes to play it by ear." Evie inspected her reflection in the mirror.

"Copper suits you, milady. It's a lovely warm shade."

"I'm not sure I agree, Caro, but I have run out of colors to wear. Let's aim for something more cheerful tomorrow, please." The distraction did not last and Evie's thoughts resumed their whirlpool of activity.

Her mind seemed to be fixated with timing. The sequence of events simply didn't add up.

According to the detective, Jacinta had returned to her office. After reading the letter Evie had sent her, she had promptly made her way to Madame Berger's fashion house.

The short distance would have been covered in under ten minutes. Jacinta should have arrived while Evie, the dowagers and Toodles were attending the fashion show. Yet Jacinta had died an hour or so later.

What had happened in the interim?

Had Jacinta visited someone else before going up to Madame Berger's salon? They knew she had been with Jacinta until just before midday. Where had she been in the time before then? With someone else?

She couldn't think of any other explanation.

Evie glanced at the clock on the bedside table. Lotte Mannering had promised to contact her as soon as she had anything of value to report. "Is there anything interesting happening downstairs?"

Caro gave it some thought. "The Reynolds have a new baby. Their fifth daughter."

"The Reynolds?"

"They're your neighbors, milady."

Evie pointed to the building next door.

"No, the other neighbors."

"Oh. How is Mrs. Reynolds?"

"Bemoaning the fact she now has to find five husbands. Or, rather, five fools to marry her daughters, which was her speech when she had her fourth daughter. She is calling it the Bennet affliction and has even named her daughters after the fictional characters. I believe she has now run out of names."

"How sad that she should feel that way," Evie murmured. "Although, perhaps she is hoping for a good outcome for at least two of them. And, who knows, one of her daughters might display a strong aptitude for estate management. They could even try to nurture their interest from an early age. In their place, I think I would do that."

"I'm afraid they are not forward thinking. Mr. Reynolds has given up hope of ever fathering a son and is now grooming his nephew to take over their country estate."

At least, Evie thought, they weren't fixated on solving a death; not something she would readily admit to doing.

Despite her efforts to make the detective's life easy by not meddling, Evie felt compelled to do what she could to assist in the investigation. In any case, the detective now seemed to be more amenable to the idea of Evie and company providing whatever information they could dig up.

This new arrangement suited Evie. They were in no hurry to return to Halton House. In fact, they could linger in town for a few more days, at least long enough to find something interesting for Seth.

Evie glanced at Caro. Her maid hadn't mentioned anything about wedding cakes. A good sign, she thought. Although, that didn't necessarily mean everyone had forgotten about the photograph.

If she asked Caro about it, she would bet anything her maid would change the subject. And that, Evie thought, would only mean Caro wanted to hide the truth from her.

"I haven't made any time to speak with the housekeeper. How is she getting on?"

"Busy as ever, milady. Oh, that reminds me. Don't be surprised if Edgar is particularly formal tonight. He is trying to avoid having to answer questions about this afternoon. I can assure you, milady, he did his best to lie to the dowagers and Toodles about your whereabouts."

"It's hardly his fault. We met by sheer accident, in fact, we were bound to cross paths."

"He's worried you won't trust him with any future undercover activities."

Evie stifled an unladylike snort. Even if she wanted to escape any type of involvement with the investigation, her staff were bound to push her into it.

A light knock at her bedroom door had Caro rushing to answer it.

Tom entered. "Are you decent?" He held a book which he waved in the air. "I couldn't wait to share this with you."

"What have you found?"

"Strychnine poisoning causes convulsions and eventually death through asphyxia."

Across the city of London people were holding

conversations and none, she imagined, would come close to sounding so macabre.

"Is that what the journalist died of?" Caro asked.

Evie shivered. "Yes, I've been trying to put it out of my mind." Looking at the book Tom held, she asked, "Is that book from my library?"

"No. I asked the detective if he could point me in the right direction. I thought he might suggest talking with a medical professional. Instead, he sent a Constable over with this book."

"Why is he suddenly being so cooperative?"

"I suspect he has decided to rebel against his Superintendent. He probably weighed his options and realized the benefits of consulting with you would be more favorable than obedience to his Superintendent."

"What else did you find?"

He turned to another paragraph. "Ten to twenty minutes after exposure, the body's muscles begin to spasm, starting with the head and neck and spreading to every muscle in the body, with nearly continuous convulsions." Tom closed the book and stared at Evie. "According to Lucy, Madame Berger's receptionist, the victim walked in, stumbled, rolled her eyes back and collapsed."

"She lied."

Tom nodded. "I can't think of any other explanation. If Jacinta had been struck by these spasms before entering the building or even after leaving Adele Lawson's salon... Well, she would not have made it very far. But she somehow managed to make it all the way up to Madame Berger's fashion house."

Evie stared into space as she said, "The timing is not

right. I've been thinking of nothing else. Detective O'Neill said the strychnine had been mixed with the cocaine. The dosage must have been fatal, with one inhalation enough to kill her very quickly. How long did you say before it takes effect?"

"Ten to twenty minutes, depending on the dosage."

"I wonder if she inhaled the cocaine before leaving the office or just after leaving Adele Lawson's salon."

Tom nodded. "Or, as you said, if the amount of strychnine was high enough to kill her quickly, just before entering Madame Berger's salon..."

Evie stopped blinking. "Either way, I think it's safe to continue to assume Madame Berger and Lucy lied. We haven't spoken with Louisa Barclay, but I'm assuming she'll lie right along with them. No one mentioned anything about convulsions or spasms. Why would they withhold that information?"

He again nodded. "I must admit, I am not having any trouble entertaining the darkest thoughts. I'm thinking Jacinta went into convulsions and they delayed contacting the authorities."

"Heavens."

"I'm not saying they did it on purpose," Tom clarified. "Of course, the possibility exists. However, Madame Berger and her staff might have been shocked by the sight and been slow to take action."

"Too shocked to try to save someone's life?" Evie frowned. "I think you are being too kind in giving them the benefit of the doubt. They must have lied to the police to cover their tracks. But for what reason? To spare themselves the embarrassment of coming across as being too dull-witted? Or did they want to make sure

Jacinta didn't receive medical assistance? That would be inhumane."

"I assume the criminal mind usually lacks humanity," Tom reasoned.

Evie looked at the title on the spine. "Strychnine Poisoning: Recent cases and studies."

Tom turned to the back pages. "In 1905, Jane Stanford, the co-founder of Stanford University and wife of California governor Leland Stanford, died from strychnine poisoning. Her murderer was never identified."

"That's not very comforting."

"Milady, I do hope you are taking care. Please, don't accept any food or beverages from anyone other than the people you know and trust."

Evie tried to lighten the moment by laughing.

"I don't find it at all amusing, milady. What if you happen to get close to the truth? The killer is bound to try anything."

"Don't fret, Caro. I'll take care. Put the book down, Tom. We should try to take our minds off the subject tonight. My thoughts are already muddled. We can't have you being muddled too."

They made their way to the drawing room. Before entering, Evie hesitated. "By the way, I think Edgar might need to be reassured. Apparently, he feels he let me down this afternoon."

Tom followed his easy smile with a slight roll of the eyes.

"Yes, I know what you must be thinking. I'm pandering to everyone's whims and sensibilities. Doesn't it make you feel guilty for teasing me?"

"Let me think..." After a brief pause, he said. "No."

"Is this what it's going to be like when we're married?"

"Bantering and teasing?" Tom barely hid his smile when he added, "I shouldn't think so. After all, you'll be making a solemn promise to obey me."

"I think this might be the time for me to become a thoroughly modern woman."

They walked into the middle of a lively conversation.

"Evangeline. You missed our unexpected guest."

Seeing their faces lit up with excitement, Evie braced herself. Martin Gate had been their last unexpected guest and that had turned into quite a night. "You all look excited."

"That's because we are." Henrietta clapped her hands. "We are going to a jazz club tonight."

"We are?" Evie settled down on a chair and accepted a drink from Edgar who appeared to be avoiding eye contact.

"A Martini, my lady."

"Thank you, Edgar. You always do such a splendid job of it."

He inclined his head and retreated to prepare a drink for Tom.

Evie took a sip of her Martini before asking, "Why are we going to a jazz club, Henrietta?"

"Lotte Mannering did a splendid job of..." Henrietta clicked her fingers as if trying to think of the right word. "Staking out the place, I believe she said. She has been busy questioning people and managed to establish Louisa Barclay's routine. It seems she has a *hang-out* and can be found there every other day. Today just happens to be the other day."

"How fortunate for us." Evie cast a cautious glance Tom's way. "Which club are we going to?"

"*Frolics*!"

Evie thought she heard Tom groan under his breath.

"I see. And where is Mrs. Mannering now?"

"She returned to her office to change into another disguise."

"I take it she will be joining us at *Frolics* in a disguise."

"Of course. She might need our support."

Both Sara and Toodles nodded in agreement.

"What exactly are we going to do at the jazz club?" Evie asked.

"You need to speak with Louisa Barclay and we think the venue will give you an advantage," Henrietta explained. "You'll have to make it look as though you bumped into her by accident."

"I see." Evie finished her drink and considered asking Edgar for another one when she realized she would need all her faculties. "What sort of advantage?"

"She'll be surprised to see you there."

"Have any of you ever been to a jazz club?" it occurred to ask.

They all shook their heads.

"We can't wait. Apparently, it will be full of flappers and bright young things." The dowager looked up at Edgar. "Do please hurry and announce dinner."

"Henrietta, these clubs don't come alive until very late in the evening," Evie warned.

"Edgar," Henrietta called out before the butler could

exit the drawing room. "Could you bring some strong coffee, please?"

Catching Tom's attention, Evie signaled for him to sit closer to her. "I get the feeling you have some reservations about this outing."

"And you don't?" he asked.

Should she be worried? "What could possibly go wrong?"

Tom sat back and tapped his chin. "Let's see... Frolics became popular with people searching for somewhere to drink and dance after the pubs closed. Frolics and other clubs like it tend to receive a great deal of police attention because they sell liquor illegally out of hours." Tom lowered his voice and murmured, "I also believe it has attracted surveillance from British Intelligence because Frolics has become the favorite night haunt of female spies in London."

"Really?"

He nodded. "It is alleged that these women have been trying to become acquainted with upper class gentlemen in the hope of recruiting them to their cause."

"So, in actual fact, you will be the only one under threat."

"I suppose, if you put it like that."

Evie patted his hand. "Don't worry, Tom. The dowagers, Toodles and I will watch your back."

CHAPTER 18

"I HAVE NEVER DONE anything so daring or adventurous," Henrietta declared as Edmonds slowed down and waited for another motor car to clear the way so he could pull up outside Frolics. "I wonder if anyone will recognize us. Heavens, we might become the hot topic of conversation."

"Let's just hope we're not mistaken for spies," Evie teased.

Sara straightened her necklace. "I hope we're suitably dressed for the occasion."

"We can't go wrong with evening dresses, Sara. Of course, you could always hitch up your dress to make it shorter," Henrietta suggested.

Toodles laughed. "I think we should be ready to turn a few heads. All for the wrong reasons. Do people our age attend these clubs?"

"If they don't, they soon will," Tom said. "You might all be responsible for starting a new trend among your contemporaries."

"I'm sure I don't need to remind you we are only here to serve as possible witnesses and offer Lotte our support," Evie explained. "Lotte Mannering will have everything under control and she will do her best to get some information. Needless to say, if we recognize her, we shouldn't give her away." Evie doubted the lady detective would get anything of value from Louisa Barclay. Since Madame Berger and her receptionist had both given a less than satisfactory version of events, Evie imagined Louisa Barclay would stick to the same story, or worse, clam up.

Then again...

Lotte Mannering had years of experience to guide her. She might be able to succeed where she and Tom had failed.

"You seem to be very preoccupied with your thoughts, Birdie. What are you thinking?"

"I'd just been entertaining a highly presumptuous thought and being quite hard on myself. While Tom and I failed to wring the truth out of Madame Berger, we did manage to establish the fact she had lied."

Sara gave a pensive nod. "There's a lesson in there for all of us. We do tend to be too harsh on ourselves when, in fact, we should focus on our strengths."

"It's human nature to focus on weaknesses and failings," Henrietta offered. "Yes, indeed. We should all try to enjoy ourselves tonight and not think we are too old to be in such a place. I might even get up and dance." Glancing at Tom, she gave him a teasing smile. "If someone will ask me."

Edmonds held the door open and they all piled out of the Duesenberg. A group of young flappers, no older than twenty years, Evie guessed, danced all the way to the front door ahead of them.

Henrietta's step faltered. "Are we supposed to make an exuberant entrance too?"

Tom, who'd been rather quiet during the short journey, laughed. "I believe it's optional."

Evie scanned the street for signs of Lotte only to tell herself the lady detective wouldn't risk revealing their association in public. Being new to this game of intrigue, she hoped she didn't do something to jeopardize the ruse.

"Did Lotte Mannering say anything about how she planned to approach us?" Evie asked. For all they knew, Lotte might have decided to disguise herself as a waiter with a curly moustache.

"She warned us to employ the utmost discretion and she would do the same and only make contact with us if she needed our assistance."

A couple of men dressed in tailcoats made their way to the entrance, chatting excitedly with their female companions who were dressed in glittering evening dresses that barely reached their knees.

"Evangeline, you and Tom should lead the way. I'm feeling slightly outside my usual milieu."

The doorman tipped his hat, gave them a brilliant smile and, holding the door open, wished them a good evening.

Evie scrutinized him and decided he was too tall to be Lotte Mannering in disguise.

"Thank heavens," Sara murmured. "For a moment there, I thought we might be turned away."

"You always tend to worry unnecessarily, Sara. Take a

deep breath and lighten your step. I'm sure you'll be tapping your foot to the rhythm of the music in no time." Despite sounding confident, Henrietta turned to Evie and whispered, "Try to look lively. You'll need to be the life of the party, Evangeline. We'll shadow your every step and hopefully no one will notice us."

Tom whispered, "Are you tempted to lead them on a merry dance?"

"If I do that," Evie whispered back, "I'm afraid I won't be able to restrain them." Observing the group ahead of them, she added, "You might have to slip that man a few bills. He appears to be some sort of gate-keeper. With our luck, he probably only allows happy people inside."

"It's all been taken care of," Tom assured her. "I telephoned ahead and organized a membership."

"You have to be a member?"

"Yes, it's the only way these types of clubs can obtain their liquor licenses."

Tom had a brief word with an immaculately dressed maître d' and they were waved through a set of double doors that took them into another world.

Lively music mingled with laughter and a hundred conversations. The lights were dim, which would make identifying Lotte Mannering difficult, Evie thought.

Henrietta pressed her hand to her throat. "My heart is thumping and I'm suddenly feeling apprehensive and excited at the same time."

They were shown through to a table with a perfect view of the dance floor and the jazz band. As soon as they sat down, a waiter rushed toward them.

Before Evie had a chance to properly settle into her

chair, the waiter rushed off again only to return with a bottle of champagne and glasses.

Evie must have shown her surprise at such speedy service because Sara and Henrietta both pointed at Toodles who said, "You were all busy settling down, the waiter is run off his feet and we have bigger things to worry about. We're all having champagne."

Evie cast a worried look around them. "Maybe this wasn't such a great idea. We can't even talk about the case because someone might hear us."

Tom handed her a glass of champagne. "Nonsense. This is the perfect place. Everyone's talking. What's on your mind?"

"I'm still obsessing about the timing. What happened between the time Jacinta left her office and then arrived at Madame Berger's salon? I can only see a huge gap. Also, I'd like to know how Jacinta came into possession of the cocaine. Either she had the cocaine contaminated with poison with her or she stopped somewhere along the way. We only know two facts. She went to her office, then to Adele Lawson's and then to Madame Berger's salon. If the killer is someone from her office, that limits the suspects to three people. The receptionist, the other journalist and the owner, Margaret Thornbury."

"You haven't included Madame Berger as a suspect. I expected her to be at the top of your list."

"I really don't see her as a supplier of cocaine. As for Adele Lawson... She's a young designer. Why would she want to kill the person she hoped would write a favorable article about her?" Evie tapped her chin. "Then there's Louisa Barclay. She was with Madame

Berger when Jacinta died. So that puts her in the clear."

Tom didn't look convinced. He leaned in and lowered his voice. "Does it? For all we know, Louisa Barclay was Jacinta's supplier and she gave herself the perfect alibi."

"You're right," Evie agreed. "Also, we don't know what happened after we left. In fact, that's when Louisa could have met with Jacinta. Perhaps we should focus on motive." She scanned the crowd but didn't find any inspiration. "Someone wanted her out of the way and they were desperate enough to kill her. What if we are on the right track and this is all about Jacinta writing that dreadful article? She only wrote one but she might have been planning a whole string of them. Killing her might have been the only way to put a stop to her disparaging articles."

"It would be a supremely cunning plan," Tom said. "Think about it. Unless a witness comes forward, it will be near impossible for the detective to find out where Jacinta went before she finally ended up at Madame Berger's. She could have stopped anywhere. And, if she had the cocaine with her all along, then the police will have to find her supplier or someone who had access to her cocaine."

Agreeing, Evie thought they needed to focus on who would gain the most by her death. "So, who has the strongest motive?"

"That we know of?"

Evie nodded. "If the magazine is losing advertisers, that could be a reason to kill Jacinta. The detective would have to find out if the canceled advertisements is something new. For all we know, the loss of revenue could be an ongoing factor, something that is a given in the publishing business." Evie took a sip of her champagne. "I wonder if the younger designers had issues with Jacinta. They might have seen her as a threat; someone who could make or break their careers."

Instead of raising his voice to be heard, Tom leaned in even closer. "Finding her cocaine supplier remains at the top of the list, but as you said, the person responsible for poisoning her cocaine might have been someone she knew and had regular contact with."

"If Lotte Mannering managed to establish Louisa Barclay's routine, surely she can do the same for Jacinta McKay. I suspect people will be more willing to share information about her movements now that she is dead."

"Given enough time, I'm sure Lotte could do that," Tom agreed.

Evie grabbed his arm. "There she is."

"Who?"

"Louisa Barclay." Evie had been scanning the crowds and hadn't managed to spot Lotte, but she had to be somewhere. "She's sitting near the bar with a redheaded lady wearing a blue dress." And, Evie thought, looking quite obvious because, unlike everyone at the nightclub, Louisa looked rather downcast.

Tom lifted the glass of champagne to his lips. "The woman in blue is either giving her advice or trying to talk her away from the ledge. Louisa looks upset."

"I just entertained a similar thought."

Tom smiled. "We appear to be working in tandem."

"I suppose if we keep our eyes on them, we'll eventually see Lotte. She might be standing near them as we speak."

Tom nearly choked on his drink.

"You didn't. Surely you didn't just imagine Lotte parading around as the woman in blue."

"I'm afraid I did. Don't ask me how. Lotte Mannering must be at least ten years older."

"If Louisa Barclay gets up to dance, you'll have to take me for a spin around the dance floor. We could pretend to bump into her," Evie suggested.

"I thought we were not going to interfere with Lotte's plans."

"Thank you for reminding me." Evie didn't wish to admit to feeling slightly on edge, almost as if they were on the brink of discovering something and they needed to forge ahead. If they gave up now, who knew what they might miss out on discovering?

She glanced over at the dowagers and Toodles. All three sat with slightly widened eyes, captivated by the dancers.

Henrietta's voice rose above the buzz of conversation around them. "It all seems to require so much energy."

"I hope it's not too much for you, Henrietta."

The dowager laughed. "Oh, my dear, Evangeline. I hide behind this veneer of absolute respectability when, in fact, I witnessed Maud Allan's *The Vision of Salomé*."

"When was that?" Evie asked.

"1908. She wore a jeweled breastplate and a transparent skirt." Henrietta made a swaying motion with her hand. "Her body swayed like an enchantress, twisting like a snake and panting..." Henrietta laughed.

"Heavens, I was about to say she panted with passion. *Oh*, I believe I just did. Did you know, several theaters barred her performance as indecent?"

Before Evie could answer, Toodles said, "I have studied everyone within sight. Either Lotte Mannering hasn't arrived yet or she has done a splendid job of disguising herself."

Tom grabbed hold of Evie's hand. "Brace yourself. She's on the move."

"Who?"

"Louisa Barclay."

Evie looked toward her table and saw her getting up and walking away.

"She's not leaving. The exit is in the opposite direction," Tom said.

"She might be going to powder her nose," Sara suggested.

The dowagers and Toodles made a move to get up.

"What are you doing?" Evie gestured for them to sit down again.

"Someone has to follow her," Toodles said.

Yes, Evie thought. Someone, but not everyone. "I'll go."

As Evie moved away from the table, Tom held up her little handbag. "You might want to take this with you. After all, you can't powder your nose if you don't take powder with you."

"Whatever you do, Birdie, be discreet. The woman in blue is looking around. You don't want her to notice you following Louisa to the lady's restroom."

Evie wove her way around the tables and headed toward the powder room. As she neared the table where Louisa Barclay had been sitting, she looked away. She'd only recently had her photograph in the newspaper and didn't wish to be recognized by the woman in blue.

Despite several women hovering around outside the restroom, she did not encounter a line and managed to walk right in.

There were cubicles to one side and a row of mirrors on the other. That's where she found Louisa.

Evie walked past a maid wiping a mirror and made a point of looking inside her small handbag as if searching for an essential item.

Going to stand a couple of feet away from Louisa Barclay, Evie inspected her hair. Out of the corner of her eye, she sensed her looking at her, but she kept her attention on the mirror. When she finished fussing with her hair, she looked down at her purse and, as she did, she saw the maid walk past her.

"Lady Woodridge?"

Instead of answering, Evie pretended to look the other way. After a few seconds, she turned and met their suspect's gaze.

"Hello." Evie stared at Louisa Barclay for a moment, her look blank. "Oh... Have we met? I feel I know you from somewhere." Evie couldn't be sure, but she thought she heard the maid chortle.

Louisa reminded her of their encounter at Madame Berger's.

"Oh, yes." Evie pressed her hand to her throat. "My goodness. I heard about the dreadful incident. Were you present?"

Louisa's eyes widened slightly when she said, "Yes. It

shook me to the core. I've never before seen anyone die."

She didn't look shaken, Evie thought. If she'd been sitting with the lady in blue, Evie would have believed her because she'd looked sullen. Now, however, she looked bright, and she sounded chirpy.

"I believe Madame Berger had a similar reaction to the experience." Evie took the opportunity to ask her if Jacinta had said anything before dying only to meet with disappointment as Louisa repeated everything the receptionist had said, word for word. Almost as if it had been rehearsed. In fact, she ticked everything off on her fingers.

Jacinta had entered, rolled her eyes back and had then collapsed.

Turning back to study her reflection, Evie continued to fuss with her hair. "Did she ever write an article about you?" Glancing at her, Evie saw Louisa shrug and swing around, her arms spread out.

"She wanted to interview me, but she kept changing her mind," she said in a sing-song tone.

"I'm curious, did she have any issues with Madame Berger?"

Louisa tipped her head back and laughed. "You must have read the article."

"Yes, indeed. I honestly couldn't believe my eyes."

"They used to be on very good terms," Louisa revealed.

Evie tried to avoid sounding too eager. "Did something happen to change that?"

Louisa flung her arms out and swung around. "Not that I know of."

Ignoring the young woman's odd behavior, Evie said, "Oh, I assumed you were close friends with Madame Berger."

"We are."

So, if something had happened, Madame Berger would have confided in her...

From the sounds of it, Jacinta had acted without provocation. Evie then remembered the journalist had suggested someone else had been responsible.

Louisa groaned and threw her head back.

"Heavens, are you feeling well?"

Louisa laughed. "Me? Oh, yes. I'm feeling great." She performed a pirouette and, waving, sauntered out of the powder room.

Puzzled by her behavior, Evie turned to leave only to remember the maid. Digging inside her little handbag, she retrieved a few coins and handed them to the maid. Belatedly, she remembered she wasn't back home and tipping was not always required. Although, she'd sometimes noticed guests at Halton House tipping Edgar.

The maid looked at the coins in her hand and, shrugging, she slipped them into her pocket.

Evie turned to leave only to stop and turn. Narrowing her eyes, she studied the woman for a moment and then asked, "Lotte?"

The lady detective muttered something under her breath, which was drowned out by the sound of police whistles blaring over the music.

CHAPTER 19

Evie and Lotte hurried to the door and eased it open.

"Do you think it's safe to go out there?" Evie asked even as she stepped out. Slowing down, she peered around the corner and saw a chaotic scene with policemen rushing about the place and frisking the male guests.

She searched for the dowagers and Toodles and found them just as Henrietta exclaimed in a voice that carried the weight of her disdain, "This is outrageous."

Tom had his hands full trying to fend off the police officers. With his arms stretched out, he herded the dowagers and Toodles toward the exit.

"Tom seems to have everything under control." Lotte tugged her back. "I think we should stay in here, well out of the way."

"Are you sure?"

"Do you want to get trampled on?"

"No, but we can't just abandon them."

"Tom knows what he's doing."

As they hurried back inside the restroom, Evie glanced over her shoulder in time to see Henrietta swing her handbag at policeman.

Evie yelped.

She took a step forward but Lotte gave her another tug.

"What do you think is going on?"

"It's a raid. Come on. We should remain out of sight."

"Yes, I suppose so... But what are they looking for?"

"Drugs, I imagine. Or maybe the club owner didn't pay protection money."

Evie looked sufficiently puzzled for Lotte to explain, "It's a security payment to exempt them from raids."

"Yes, I understand the concept but I'm struggling to believe this establishment needs to take such measures." If she became a lady detective, she would have to learn all about raids and policemen frisking people and... "Are you serious? They extort money from club owners?"

"It's been known to happen. Although, it's not always the police. Sometimes, it's a crook demanding protection money and if they don't get what they want, they contact the police and tip them off."

Standing in the middle of the restroom, Evie exclaimed, "Dishonest crooks? What is this world coming to?"

"Precisely. And that's why being a private detective is such a lucrative business."

Hearing something crash against the wall, Evie yelped again. "I'm not sure about this. It feels rather cowardly to hide in here."

"Feel free to go out there. I'm happy to remain here until everything settles down."

"Yes, I suppose you're right. We should wait." She leaned against a basin and crossed her arms. "By the way, congratulations on your disguise. It's quite effective but how did you manage to gain access to the club?"

"I know one of the maids who works here."

"I suppose in your line of business it helps to know all sorts of people. Did you discover anything before I came in?"

Lotte nodded and signaled to one of the stalls. "I think that's a pick-up point."

"A what?"

"A delivery place. I observed several women going in and coming out sniffing and wiping their noses."

Evie gasped. "I noticed Louisa's odd behavior. Are you saying she was under the influence?"

"Yes."

Curious, Evie walked toward the corner stall and leaned in for a look inside. "I don't see anything."

"Let me have a look."

"Do you think the police will come in here?"

"If they do, scream and pull rank on them," Lotte suggested.

Evie wondered if she could pull rank without having to scream. "I suppose I can pretend to be haughty."

"I think I found something. There's a hole in the wall the size of a coin. I'm guessing there's an alley on the other side of this wall." Lotte stepped back to let Evie take a look.

"So, you think someone stood outside and handed the drugs through that hole?"

"It's possible."

"What an odd arrangement. Then again, the seller would remain anonymous."

"That's right."

Evie leaned down and whispered through the hole, "Hello?" When she didn't get an answer, she straightened and backed out. "Before you say anything, I thought it might be worth a try." Unfortunately, it didn't bring them any closer to discovering anything new about Jacinta's killer. "I don't suppose you overheard something of interest before I came in."

"No, Louisa Barclay went into the cubicle and, a moment later, she came out looking quite happy. They must have some way of arranging it all."

"On the bright side, we've made a discovery and a connection. Louisa Barclay is a cocaine user, just like Jacinta McKay." Evie glanced toward the door.

"Don't worry. The police wouldn't dare come in here."

"I wouldn't be so sure about that. They looked quite determined." Evie forced her attention away from the door. "Since we now know Louisa had access to the drug, I think she can be included in our list of suspects. It's possible she gave Jacinta the cocaine. As for motive... Well, I haven't been able to come up with anything new. You must deal with that every day. How do you cope with coming up with a dead-end?"

"It's a game of patience and observation. You either have the skill or you acquire it."

"So, one could train to become a private detective."

"Of course."

A loud thump had them both swinging toward the

door. When nothing else happened, they both shrugged and resumed their conversation.

Lotte tilted her head and studied her for a moment. "Your grandmother mentioned you wanted to go into the business."

"When did she say that?"

"Earlier today, before you arrived at my office. Of course, she thought she was talking to my imaginary receptionist..."

Evie didn't bother denying it. As Tom had pointed out, she had a keen eye for detail as well as an ability to notice things others seemed to miss. Evie actually thought she merely had a good imagination...

The ruckus outside continued. It seemed odd to carry on with their conversation but, as Lotte had pointed out, there was nothing to be gained by joining the rest of the nightclub guests.

"Until you decide what to do, you could partner up with me," Lotte suggested.

"Are you serious?"

"I don't see the harm in it. While I prefer to work alone, I can see the benefit of going into partnership with someone of your stature."

A partnership might be too much of a commitment to start with, but Evie could see herself taking an interest.

As the idea wove around her mind, she pictured herself embracing an entrepreneurial spirit and setting an example for Seth.

While his future had already been mapped out and his livelihood safeguarded, he would have to find an interest to keep him occupied. Evie couldn't expect him to devote his life to the running of the estate, and she certainly wouldn't force him into it, in any case, they had people to ensure it all worked like a well-oiled machine.

Hearing another thump against the door, Evie's voice hitched. "I'm beginning to appreciate the benefits of such a venture... So, what now?"

"Margaret Thornbury is advertising for a new staff writer."

"And you're going to apply for the job?"

"I have an interview set up for tomorrow. I'll arrive early so I can have the opportunity to talk with the receptionist and anyone else who happens to be in the office. There's bound to be some sort of information the police haven't pieced together. They might have the place under surveillance, so breaking and entering would be too risky." Lotte brushed a finger along her chin. "I might need to create a distraction."

"Oh, if you need help, I'm sure Caro and Millicent would be only too happy to step in. While you're at it, see if you can find a connection between Jacinta's life choices and Margaret Thornbury." Evie told her about the photograph she'd seen of the two women together. "Margaret says she had a working relationship, but I think there might have been more to it. I'd also like to know about Margaret Thornbury's marriage. She sounded too blasé about it. For all we know, she has a skeleton in her closet and Jacinta threatened to expose her."

"Your suspicious mind is admirable," Lotte said. "It will serve you well in this business."

Evie wouldn't get carried away, but the more she

thought about it, the more intrigued she became. "I notice you don't use a notebook."

Lotte tapped her head. "It's all in here."

Evie looked heavenward. "I have so much going on inside my head, I have come to rely on my trusty notebook."

The sound of someone clearing his throat had them both turning.

Evie straightened. Instead of looking surprised, she smiled. "Detective. Good evening."

The detective removed his hat. "My lady." He leaned in and narrowed his eyes. "Mrs. Mannering? Is that you?"

Lotte crossed her arms and pursed her lips. After a moment, she gave a stiff nod.

"What is this all about, detective?" Evie asked.

"Nothing but a regular inspection, my lady," he said as police whistles continued to blow. He gestured toward the door. "Permit me to escort you both out. Unless, of course, you were in the middle of an important conversation."

"As a matter of fact, detective, we were discussing the case." Evie steered the conversation in another direction. "Did you raid the very nightclub Louisa Barclay frequents on a regular basis by accident or have you been following her?"

"We actually received information about certain activities at this club."

Evie glanced at Lotte who gave a discreet shrug. "I thought it might stir things up a bit."

The detective slipped his hands inside his coat pockets. He could not have looked more pleased with himself. "I believe Miss Barclay is going to be charged with the possession of narcotics."

Lotte gave him a knowing smile. "The prospect of a night in prison is likely to loosen her tongue."

Evie remembered Louisa's version of events had sounded rehearsed. Either she and the others wanted to protect themselves because they were guilty of something or they were frightened of someone else...

"Yes, indeed. She is hiding something and I'm beginning to think she is conspiring with the others. Well done, detective. Henrietta will appreciate your tactics."

"Perhaps not if the circumstances had been reversed. Lady Woodridge came perilously close to being carted off with the rest of them."

"Heavens. On what charge?"

"Assaulting a police officer," he said as they walked out. "She clobbered one of my men with her silver handbag. I believe she employed the diversionary tactic to distract the police officer from identifying the person who kicked him in the sheen. I can't be sure, but your grandmother looked rather triumphant."

They stepped out into the continuing chaos, with a few uncooperative guests giving the police a run for their money.

"So, did you come up with any new theories, my lady?"

A woman shrieked and they all ducked in time to avoid a shoe flying across.

"Yes, I believe I have. Louisa Barclay cannot possibly be responsible for Jacinta's death. Her behavior tonight confirmed she doesn't possess the cold and calculating temperament of a killer. In fact, I see her as a loose cannon so you might be in luck, detective. If she knows something, I think she will reveal it under pressure."

Evie decided to leave it up to Lotte to inform the detective about her discovery. "Unless you have any more questions, I think I should make sure Henrietta doesn't end up spending the night in one of your cells." Turning to Lotte, she asked, "Would you like us to drive you somewhere?"

"Thank you for the offer but I left my motor car nearby."

When two police officers jostled past them, the detective apologized to Evie and took her arm. "I'll escort you to your motor car, my lady."

"Thank you, detective. That's very kind. I expect Tom to come rushing in at any moment. I'm so glad the dowagers and Toodles had him looking after them." Evie suspected no one would want to retire for the evening just yet as they'd all want to share their experiences with her.

Ahead of them, the doors to the club burst open and the two police officers exited with their charge kicking and screaming.

"I must say, I'm glad the dowagers and my granny were here to see this. If I'd told them about it, they would not have believed me."

Stepping out of the nightclub, Evie saw a crowd had gathered to watch the excitement with some people pushing and elbowing their way to gain a better vantage point.

Evie scanned the street and saw several police wagons. As she pulled her gaze away, something caught her attention. Her eyes sprung back to see Louisa Barclay, her fingers curled around the iron bars on the police wagon.

When she spotted Evie, she called out her name at the top of her voice. "Lady Woodridge. *Lady Woodridge.*"

Heavens, she looked miserable and desperate.

As Evie turned to the detective to suggest there might be another way of transporting poor Louisa Barclay to the police station, she was blinded by the flash of a camera.

"Oh, dear... Not again."

※

"Evangeline. We're so relieved to see you made it out of that infernal place safe and sound. Tom tried to reassure us. Apparently, he saw the detective going inside, but we couldn't rest easy until we could see you for ourselves."

"Birdie. Did they try to haul you away too?"

Sara fanned herself. "We've been so anxious, waiting for you to emerge from the club. Edmonds produced a cricket bat and stood guard to make sure those horrid policemen wouldn't pull us out of the motor car. They seemed intent on rounding up as many people as possible."

Tom shook his head. Removing a pristine white handkerchief from his pocket, he wiped his brow.

"You look out of breath, Tom" Evie remarked.

"You don't know the half of it."

"I heard something about Henrietta assaulting a police officer."

"I lost a shoe." Henrietta lifted her chin. "The policeman should have helped me search for it."

Toodles grinned. "Sara managed to sucker-punch one of them."

Evie's lips parted. *Sara?*

Her mother-in-law looked quite pleased.

"Toodles exaggerates. I merely poked him with my finger. Now I fear we will wake up to fresh headlines. The notorious dowagers and their American counterpart raising hell at a scandalous nightclub."

Evie didn't want to mention the possibility she might once again make the front page. Although, they might end up sharing the front-page podium.

It almost felt as if the Fates were conspiring against her by forcing her to step out into the limelight.

"Drive on, Edmonds. There's nothing more for us to see here."

"Does that mean you saw something, Birdie?"

Laughing, Evie told them about Lotte Mannering's disguise. "She put so much effort into her disguise but even the detective managed to identify her."

They traveled the rest of the way talking over each other, their excitement suggesting they were actually savoring their experiences and, if given the opportunity, would do it all over again.

CHAPTER 20

The next morning...

EVIE LOOKED up from her breakfast and thought she saw Edgar trying to contain his laughter but she couldn't be sure because he immediately straightened and adopted the disinterested look he'd honed to perfection.

She resumed buttering her toast only to lower her knife. "I keep forgetting to ask if Martin Gate printed a retraction." Fearing the worst, she hadn't bothered with the newspaper that morning. "And I think I'm doing it on purpose. A part of me just doesn't want to know."

Tom lowered his newspaper and shook his head. "I haven't come across one. However..."

"Yes?"

Tom set the newspaper aside. "It can wait until later."

"But I'm intrigued now." She glanced away and saw Edgar looking up at the ceiling. "If I had to guess, I'd say Edgar knows about whatever it is you want to say."

"He might."

"Is it about Jacinta?"

"No."

"Then... Oh, for heaven's sake, if my picture has been plastered on the front page, I might as well see it now."

"You didn't actually make the front page." Tom reached for the newspaper and was about to hand it over when the door to the morning room burst open and Henrietta hurried in.

Stopping at the head of the table, Henrietta drew in a sharp breath and announced, "My dear Evangeline. I have brought disrepute and shame to the good name of Woodridge. How will I ever live this down?"

"Henrietta! What's happened?"

"Millicent woke me up this morning with the news. I'm afraid we will have to make a discreet return to Halton House. I don't dare show my face in the village, at least not until this business has died down." Henrietta shuddered. "Something that is not likely to happen any time soon as people seem to have long memories. I might now be forced to lead a reclusive life. We will definitely have to take the back road into Halton House. I wouldn't be surprised if we find the entire village waiting at the gates for our arrival. Or worse, at the train station."

Thinking Henrietta's melodramatic announcement might have something to do with the day's headline, Evie reached for the newspaper.

Scanning the front page, she gasped.

The dowagers and Toodles had been captured right at the moment when they had ganged up on a police officer.

Evie narrowed her eyes and tilted her head. "Is Toodles trying to bite his ear off?"

"I believe so," Tom said. "When the first whistle blew, they seemed to reach a mutual decision to stand united. In their defense, the police officers were not watching where they were going and pushed past us."

"We were provoked." Henrietta could not have sounded more indignant. "No manners whatsoever. Pushing us like cattle..."

Evie looked at Tom. "And where were you during this scuffle?"

Tom leaned forward and pointed at the corner of the photograph. "I believe that's my hand reaching for the police officer's neck to pull him back."

"Yes, if not for Tom, we might all have spent the night in a prison cell." Henrietta shuddered. "You'd think the police would be too busy with real criminals to bother with the likes of us."

"I don't know, Henrietta. It looks like their actions might have been justified. But how did you all manage to get free? The photograph shows two other officers lunging for you."

"Tom recognized one of them. Apparently, they served together. Just picture it if you can. Right in the middle of the melee, they both stopped, straightened their shoulders and saluted each other." Forgetting her admission of guilt, Henrietta helped herself to a piece of toast and sat next to Tom. "Unless we have some other pressing matters to attend to, I think I will sit down and write a letter of complaint to the Superintendent. Imagine what young Seth will think if he sees the photograph?"

"Does it mention your name?" Evie had a closer look at the picture. "Heavens, it does and the photograph is surprisingly clear." Her eyes narrowed as she noticed something else.

"Has something caught your attention, Countess?" Tom asked.

"Yes. Yes, indeed." She showed him the photograph. "Does that look like Adele Lawson to you?"

"Why, yes... Do you think she was at the club last night?"

Evie continued studying the photograph. "She's standing with all the spectators and she's wearing a coat."

Tom suggested, "She could have been making her way to the club."

Evie gave a pensive shake of her head. "She's wearing lace-up shoes. No, it doesn't look like she was dressed for a night out on the town."

Tom had a closer look. "Yes, you might be right and I know how you feel about coincidences."

"Yes, this is too much of a coincidence."

Sara and Toodles walked in and greeted everyone. When they didn't say anything about the photograph, Henrietta drew their attention to it.

Sara sighed. "I suppose there is no point in asking Martin Gate to print a retraction. The proof is right there in black and white."

"I suggest we keep a low profile." Henrietta took a

quick sip of her tea. "Or, we could do something else to create a distraction. I'm sure if the three of us put our heads together we'll be able to come up with something." Brightening, Henrietta asked, "What is on the agenda this morning?"

"As you suggested, you might want to keep a low profile today. Tom and I will pay a visit to Adele Lawson. We have the perfect excuse to visit her. She is making my wedding gown."

The dowager's eyebrows lifted incrementally. "When did this happen? Never mind that. Will I need to get a new outfit?"

Toodles smiled. "By the sounds of it, we might all need a new outfit, just in case."

"Anyhow," Evie continued, "Caro and Millicent will be assisting Lotte in her investigation today. I believe they will be creating a diversion for Lotte."

Sipping her coffee, Evie focused on Adele Lawson. She could not have been at the club by coincidence. Two possibilities occurred to her. Setting her cup down, she excused herself and went to the library to find her notebook.

After filling several pages with notes and doodles, she stood up and stretched just as the door to the library opened and Caro stepped in.

"Milady. I just wanted to tell you Millicent and I are ready to leave."

It took Evie a moment to remember her maids had been engaged to participate in Lotte's investigation.

"Is there anything you need before we go?"

"No, Caro. Do take care."

Caro smiled from ear to ear. "We will, milady."

Evie turned back to her notes and, retrieving a fresh notebook from her drawer, she sat down and filled another few pages, this time with thoughts about Margaret Thornbury.

Hearing the door to the library opening again, Evie looked up at the clock on the mantlepiece.

Heavens. She had been scribbling down her thoughts for nearly an hour.

With her pen hovering over Adele's name, she glanced over her shoulder and saw Tom enter the library.

Greeting him, she returned to her notes and, without giving it much thought, she drew a line connecting Adele Lawson to an unidentified cocaine seller.

"Heavens." If asked to explain her reasoning, she would not know what to say other than... "It would be so outrageous, you just never know."

Tom plumped up a cushion and sat down on a sofa.

Reading through her notes, Evie asked in a distracted tone, "What have you been doing?"

"As you pointed out, I had been grinding my back teeth, so I decided to do something about it."

"Oh? What did you do? Fill your mouth with cotton wool?"

Tom laughed. "No, I found a new motor car."

"Since I'm not surprised, I should ask, what took you so long to find such a simple solution?"

"You've kept me rather busy running around the place." He leaned his head back and looked up at the ceiling. "It's red. I hope the color doesn't clash with your clothes."

"Red. That sounds rather dangerous and fast. Is it a roadster?"

"Of course, and it's just begging to be taken for a long drive." He stretched his legs out and crossed them at the ankles. "Have you made any headway?"

"I've been busy jotting down every thought that crossed my mind. My head feels lighter so it might have worked as a purge."

"What were you saying when I came in?"

Evie hummed under her breath. "I'd been trying to gain a better understanding of Adele Lawson."

Tom drummed his fingers on the armrest. "She's not easily fooled. Remember, it took some doing to convince her you really wanted her to design a dress for you. Let's see... What else? She's young and yet, she appears to be doing quite well. How does one set up a fashion house in such a prime position?"

"I would imagine one would need an abundance of funding. Or an alternative way of making money."

"Are you imagining her as a drug trafficker? It wouldn't be beyond the realm of possibilities. Remember, not long ago, we encountered the drug trafficking ring using a dressmaker as a front."

Evie set down her pen and, getting up, walked to the window. "I'm actually thinking we should be more creative. From the start, I've been trying to imagine what the killer's motive might be. What if the killer doesn't have one?"

Tom straightened. Shifting to the edge of his seat, he gave her his full attention.

Glancing over her shoulder, Evie saw him running his fingers along his chin.

"That would make the killer a bad seed," he mused.

"Evil," she agreed. "A cold-blooded murderer, intent on causing havoc for his own amusement."

"You're picturing a man rather than a woman?"

Evie looked down at the floor and drew a circle with the tip of her shoe. "I'm trying to avoid jumping to obvious conclusions but, you make a valid point. After all, all our suspects are women. And one of them feels quite confident." Evie bit the edge of her lip. "Of course, it's all nonsense. The killer must have a reason for getting rid of Jacinta." Had they feared they might become Jacinta's next target?

"Have you heard from Lotte?" Tom asked.

"No, I haven't. I hope it's all going well for her. In hindsight, I just can't see Margaret Thornbury killing Jacinta. If the articles she wrote were responsible for the loss of advertisers, Margaret could have simply fired her."

"Yes, but... What if Jacinta had been blackmailing her? Remember, you think there might have been more to their relationship."

Evie sat down. "You're right. There's also the remark she made when I met her coming out of Madame Berger's building. *It's not me you should be talking to*. I still can't figure out what she meant by that." Evie pressed a finger to her lips. "Oh."

"Oh?"

"In my youth, I knew this girl who never accepted responsibility for anything. She would always pass the buck. Nothing was ever her fault." Evie sprung to her feet. "We know Jacinta enjoyed certain perks. We've also played around with the idea Madame Berger might have refused to pay up. Jacinta then goes ahead and writes a derogatory article. Not because she wanted to but rather because her hand had been forced by Madame Berger's lack of cooperation."

"That's a sound theory. Unfortunately, you haven't narrowed the list of suspects."

Evie puffed up a cushion and sat down next to Tom. "No, in fact, we have one more. Adele Lawson." Shaking her head, she added, "The killer will simply have to make a mistake."

"But in order for that to happen, we would have to provoke them."

"Yes, I suppose so. It might be enough to simply continue to ask questions."

When the telephone rang, they both stilled.

"How odd," Evie said. "I don't think I've ever heard it ring."

Before either one of them could get up to answer the telephone, it stopped ringing.

"Either they grew impatient and disconnected the call or Edgar answered it on the other line."

The sound of hurried footsteps had them both swinging toward the door.

Evie didn't wait for it to open. She shot to her feet and braced herself.

The door burst open. Edgar held on to the doorknob, his knuckles showing white. He swayed on the spot and struggled to catch his breath. Finally, he managed to say, "Seth. *It's Seth.*" Pressing his hand to his chest, he drew in a breath. "There's been an accident."

CHAPTER 21

Half an hour into the drive, Evie continued to berate herself for sending Seth to a preparatory boarding school at such a young age.

Oh, why had she succumbed to pressure from those who'd claimed they knew best?

She leaned forward and grabbed hold of the dashboard.

"That won't make the car go any faster." Despite raising his voice, the sound of the powerful engine nearly drowned out Tom's words.

"Are you sure? What about the law of dynamics?" Evie asked.

"What about it?"

"I don't know. I just assume if I put my weight forward... Oh, never mind. Just... Just hurry."

She'd never seen Edgar lose his composure. With him at the helm, everything always ran smoothly. Without him, the entire household would fall apart.

Seconds after he'd broken the news, Tom and Evie

had jumped into action, a single thought driving them onwards. They needed to get to Seth.

Shock had reverberated throughout the household with everyone rushing around in a mad panic. Hats and coats had been fetched. The dowagers and Toodles had alternated between falling into a stunned silence to talking over each other.

As they'd driven off, Evie had looked over her shoulder. Everyone had stood on the front steps, their mouths gaping open, their eyes wide as Tom had put the pedal to the metal.

Before Evie could ask, he'd said, "An hour. We'll be there in an hour."

That meant they were now half way there.

An accident.

Edgar hadn't been given any other details and they had been in too much of a panic to stop to ask questions he couldn't answer.

Had Seth been injured? She knew he would be well looked after. The school masters would have acted with swift promptness, calling in a doctor, if necessary. She wished the person who had placed the telephone call had provided more information.

This couldn't possibly be life threatening. Surely, if the news had been worse, they would have asked to speak with her.

Evie gave a firm nod.

"Relax. It's probably nothing more than a knee scrape. Well, maybe it's something slightly more serious, but if that's the case, they would have said something, they would have given you more information." Tom's reasoning echoed her own thoughts. He gave a firm nod. "Yes, they would have insisted on speaking with you."

"I'm fine, Tom. I just wish we could be there now."

Tom gripped the steering wheel and put his head down. Evie didn't think the motor car could go any faster but it seemed to do just that.

Despite her impatience to get there, she refused to let panic set in. Children fell from trees and horses all the time. They tumbled around and engaged in playful tussles that didn't always turn out well.

An accident, she reasoned, suggested there had not been a deliberate intention to cause harm.

When the town came into view, she told herself they were only a few minutes away from their destination. Yet, five minutes later, the town appeared to be further away.

Evie forced herself to close her eyes, saying she wouldn't open them until they arrived.

"Brace yourself." Tom slammed on the breaks and came to a screeching halt. Evie took a peek and saw they'd stopped right outside the school gates.

Tom jumped out of the motor car. When no one came out of the gatekeeper's house, he pressed his hand against the car horn.

A window opened and a man waved to them. Eventually, he emerged from the gatekeeper's cottage and, fumbling with a large set of keys, came to a stop to ask what business they had at the school.

Tom identified himself and Evie.

Saying he needed to telephone the main house, the gatekeeper trudged back to the cottage.

Evie looked beyond the gates and across the well-tended gardens and lawns surrounding the building. The times she came to visit Seth, she always saw children running about the place, either enjoying recreational activities or rushing to get to their classrooms. Now there wasn't a single soul in sight.

It felt like an eternity before the gatekeeper returned and opened the gate.

"The pupils are all at choir practice. You will be met at the front door." The gate screeched open and he waved them through.

"This doesn't feel right." Evie scanned the grounds. A few birds swooped around and flitted about on the lawns.

If something had happened, there would be people around. Also, the gatekeeper would have been warned of their imminent arrival.

Tom sped along, leaving a trail along the recently raked pebbled drive. Switching gears, he slowed down, but only just as he once again came to another screeching halt.

They were both out of the roadster and rushing up the steps just as the front door opened and a schoolmaster dressed entirely in black stepped out.

He greeted them with extended arms and a wide smile. "Lady Woodridge. What a pleasure it is to see you."

Despite meeting him on several occasions, Evie couldn't remember his name. "Seth." She gasped. "The Earl of Woodridge."

Tom took over from Evie and demanded to be taken straight to him.

The schoolmaster looked utterly perplexed.

Tom responded by gnashing his teeth. His fingers curled into tight fists. Evie put a placating hand on his and found the words to explain why they had rushed to the school.

"There appears to be some sort of misunderstanding. If anyone made such a call, it would be me and I can assure you, my lady, I did not. The Earl of Woodridge is safe and sound and, at this moment, attending his choir practice."

Despite the assurances, they needed to see him with their own eyes and so insisted on being escorted to the chapel.

They watched Seth from a distance. Evie wanted to rush to him and throw her arms around him but common sense prevailed.

The panic she had been trying her best to ignore continued to rush through her. She wouldn't be surprised if she still looked in shock.

"We don't want to alarm him," Evie managed to say.

"Forgive me for saying so, my lady, but if this is a hoax, then it is in very poor taste."

When he offered them refreshments, Evie thanked him but declined the invitation saying they needed to return to town.

She looked at Tom. "Before we leave, we'll need to telephone the others and let them know..."

"I'll take care of it."

Evie headed back to the roadster, while Tom followed the schoolmaster to his office.

Her thoughts tumbled around her mind as the panic that had taken a hold of her eased away and she tried to figure out what had happened.

Had someone tried to get them out of the way?

A few minutes later, Tom emerged from the main building. "I had no trouble picturing their response. Everyone must have been gathered around Edgar waiting to hear some news. I heard a collective sigh of relief followed by cheers."

Tom walked around the motor car and took care of checking the fuel and tires.

Evie could see his jaw muscles clenching and unclenching and imagined him wishing to get his hands on the person responsible for putting everyone through such an awful ordeal.

When he finally settled down beside her, he pushed out a breath and said, "It seems no one can get into the school grounds without being noticed."

"That's reassuring."

They both sat back and stared at the school building.

After several minutes, Evie broke the silence. "I don't want to frighten Seth. Being rational is not easy, but I think we should wait until we can all see him... When this is all over."

"I agree."

Evie went on to say, "Something tells me Seth isn't in any danger. For starters, why would anyone want to hurt him? What would they gain by it? Revenge?" Shaking her head, she added, "This isn't about me or us. Although, in a strange way, it might be."

Tom stared into the distance toward the chapel. "Do you suppose someone wanted to get us out of the way?"

"Yes, but why now? Why today? Is it possible we did something to push the killer into taking action?"

Tom tapped his finger on the steering wheel. "What if we encountered the killer and inadvertently said something?"

Evie ran through all the people they had recently met. Shifting on her seat to face him, her eyes widened with surprise. "My encounter with Louisa Barclay last night was rather unusual. Do you think she is responsible for making the telephone call?"

"Maybe. However, she might still be in custody."

"The only other person I can think of is Adele Lawson," Evie suggested. "Her presence outside the club last night struck me as rather strange. She went there for a reason other than to have a good time." She raised her hand to brush her fingers across her brow and saw her fingers trembling slightly. "What sort of person would be capable of such a heartless act?"

"Someone with a twisted mind."

"If the person responsible went to all this trouble, then they must think we can somehow connect them to Jacinta's murder."

"That's right."

"And they would want us out of the way because they think we know something and might pass on the information to the police."

"You think they wanted to buy themselves some time?" Tom shrugged. "Lotte is with Margaret Thornbury. So, that leaves Madame Berger and we don't think her capable of murder. Lying? Yes. Murder, not so much. Then, there's Adele Lawson."

Evie straightened. "I'm fine with assuming it's Adele Lawson. Do you think she tried to buy herself some time to make her escape?" In the next breath, she said,

"But that would be utterly stupid. We could have told the detective about our suspicions last night or early this morning." Evie looked around and behind them, toward the road.

"I hope you're not thinking she might try to get rid of us."

"Sending us on a wild goose chase would be one way of mapping our whereabouts. It would be easy to set someone up along the road to take a shot at us."

Tom gave her a raised eyebrow look. "Thinking like a villain seems to come second nature to you."

"I prefer to think I have a creative mind." Evie scooped in a breath. "Let's head back to town but first, I think you should telephone the detective and let him know what's happened. He might be able to take action."

As Evie waited, she realized how torn she felt. A part of her thought she should stay and make sure nothing happened to Seth. Clearly, they were dealing with a disturbed person.

She decided to wait for Tom to return before suggesting taking further measures to ensure Seth remained safe.

Moments later, she saw Tom hurrying out of the building, his fingers curling and uncurling.

"The detective will contact the local constabulary. They will keep an eye on the school."

Relief swept through Evie. "And? What about the rest?"

"I told him about our suspicions."

Evie had the distinct impression Tom wanted to avoid telling her the rest.

He brushed his hands across his face. "Adele could not have made the telephone call because the detective had been talking with her at the time. In fact, he spent the morning talking with her. And Louisa Barclay has only now been released from prison."

That left Madame Berger.

Evie gave a firm nod. "We need to get moving. I feel quite helpless just sitting here."

With the motor car roaring to life, Tom tipped his hat down. "Hold on. This might be a bumpy ride."

CHAPTER 22

Evie spent the long drive back to town focused on their arrival and she became vaguely aware of the distance they had covered when Tom had to slow down.

Yet, she did not notice the traffic along Regent Street. In her mind, she saw the road cleared of all motor cars, just for them. In reality, Tom had to perform some expert maneuvering to get them to their destination.

She finally became fully conscious of their surroundings when Tom made a sharp turn into a side street and brought the motor car to a screeching halt.

The tires, she thought, would be well and truly worn out by now.

Tom pushed back his hat and looked up at the building. "What now?"

Evie's fingers curled into tight balls. She spoke through gritted teeth, "We'll start with Adele Lawson and work our way up the building. I know you said she spent the morning talking with the detective, but I'd still like to speak with her."

"You want to see how she'll react to your accusation."

"Who said anything about accusing her?"

"How else will you get a reaction from her?"

Evie couldn't help sounding defensive. "For starters, I'm going to be tactful."

"And after that?"

"I'll play it by ear. If she's guilty, she's bound to make a mistake. Then again, she might not even be here."

They walked up the steps, stony determination stamped on their faces.

Evie feared that if Adele Lawson didn't answer the knock at her door, Tom would simply kick it down. While neither one had expressed their opinions out loud, they both felt Adele had managed to hoodwink the detective.

If she did not answer...

Heavens. Had she made the telephone call to buy herself some time and make her escape?

Fortunately, Tom did not have to resort to brute force. Adele answered the door and could not have looked more surprised to see them.

Evie knew there were several ways to interpret her reaction. She chose to think Adele hadn't expected to see them so soon because, despite the detective providing an alibi for her, she had indeed been responsible for raising a false alarm.

Foregoing all pleasantries, Evie marched right in. When she reached the fireplace, she swung around to face Adele.

Tom came to stand beside her, his hands clasped behind his back, his expression looking quite stern.

Adele looked from one to the other. "Why do I get the feeling you are not pleased?"

Adele's blithe tone managed to enrage Evie. If she'd planned on employing any tactics, they were well and truly forgotten. "We saw you at the jazz club last night. What were you doing there?"

Adele crossed her arms and smiled. "When I saw the photograph this morning in the newspaper I thought it might raise some questions. In fact, the detective subjected me to a thorough line of questioning. I'll tell you what I told him. I'm embarrassed to say, I'm no better than the average person. I saw the commotion and stopped to gawk at the scene."

Unsatisfied with the response, Evie persevered. "Do you live near the jazz club?"

"No. I don't."

"So what were you doing there?" Evie didn't bother softening her tone. She sounded as hard as a rock.

"I had just been to visit a friend."

Evie harrumphed. "A likely story."

"I believe the detective has verified it by talking to my friend who has been ill for several days. I had promised to stop by with some soup and comforting words. She has only recently moved into town from a small village and doesn't know anyone."

Unwilling to accept the explanation, Evie tapped her foot. "It would be easy enough to pay someone to pretend they were sick. In fact, it would be just as easy to get them to make a telephone call." She took a step toward Adele Lawson. "You wanted us out of the way and preoccupied with something else because you thought we would connect you to Jacinta's death."

"W-why would you think that? I haven't given you any reason to think I had anything to do with her death."

"That's because you covered your tracks, but you made a mistake last night and this morning. Did Jacinta McKay threaten to write an article about you? Is that it? Is that why you killed her? I'm sure you've worked too hard to establish your business and you couldn't let her destroy you." Evie fished around for the first idea that cropped in her mind. "She wanted something and when you refused to give it to her, she threatened to do to you what she did to Madame Berger and you couldn't let that happen."

What other reason could there be?

The detective had been working on the case and he hadn't been able to find a solid lead that would provide him with a possible motive.

People didn't go around poisoning someone for no good reason. This had to be about Jacinta becoming a loose cannon and having the power to make or break a designer's career.

"Admit it. You decided to take matters into your own hands. She came to see you and, knowing she had an addiction to cocaine, you provided her with the drug, but not before adding some poison to it." Evie barely stopped to draw breath. "Is that what you were doing at the jazz club last night? Buying more drugs for the next person who dares to stand in your way? Perhaps you have me in your sights."

Adele's face paled. "My lady, you are clearly upset about something. Would you like some tea?"

"Tea? *Tea?* Do you think I'd be foolish enough to fall for that trick?" Evie expected the young designer to defend herself against the accusations. Instead, she remained calm. Until...

Her eyes glimmered and brimmed with tears.

Were they crocodile tears?

No. Evie took a step back.

They were real tears.

Adele's bottom lip trembled. Evie watched her struggle to remain composed and keep the tears at bay, but then one spilled over, followed by another and another...

Adele garbled something which Evie couldn't quite make out. She looked at Tom who shrugged.

Riddled with guilt, Evie took another step back. Although, she couldn't quite bring herself to comfort the young woman.

Too many people had told blatant lies.

What if Adele possessed the skill to cry on command?

When they'd first met her, Adele hadn't been fooled by them. In fact, she'd been suspicious of their intentions; not quite believing they wanted her to design a wedding gown. She might be young, Evie thought, but she wasn't naïve and she certainly didn't come across as being overly sensitive.

Her crying simply didn't make sense.

Evie lifted her chin a notch. She had to be putting on an act.

"If you confess now the police will go easy on you. If

you don't, be prepared to face the consequences." Evie thrust a finger out and wagged it in front of Adele's face.

The young designer could not have looked more horrified. "I have already told the police everything," she wailed and, stumbling back, she collapsed onto a chair.

Raking his fingers through his hair, Tom signaled to Evie's finger. "You can put away your weapon. I don't think you'll get a confession out of her now."

"Oh, for heaven's sake. She's putting on an act."

Adele looked up. Tears continued to stream down her face and her cheeks had turned a deep shade of crimson.

Growling, Evie felt she couldn't get out of there fast enough. She tugged Tom's sleeve and hurried out of the salon.

She didn't give herself any time to think. Instead, she pointed toward the stairs.

Tom's eyebrows shot up. "Are you going to make Louisa Barclay cry too?"

"Only as a last resort."

Halfway up the stairs, they could still hear Adele wailing. Some women managed to look pretty while crying. She had a distant cousin whose emotional outbursts only required a dainty dabbing of the corner of her eye. Adele, however, had gone from looking like a well-composed, well-dressed young woman to a thorough mess, with red blotches on her cheeks and eyes reddened by her tears.

"I suppose I will have to send her a note of apology."

Stopping outside Louisa's atelier, Evie drew in a calming breath and then knocked on the door.

She was about to knock again when the door edged open and a softly spoken young woman greeted them.

"Yes?"

"We're here to see Louisa Barclay."

"I'm afraid that's not possible. Miss Barclay is... indisposed."

Tom pressed his hand on the door and pushed it open wider.

The young woman jumped back. "Sir!"

They both took a step inside only to stop at the sight of Louisa stretched out on a couch, her arm thrown over her face.

"Miss Barclay had a difficult night," the young woman explained.

"When did she arrive?" Evie demanded.

"Not so loud, please. She arrived only a short while ago."

And she still wore the previous night's gown, Evie noticed.

"She came in to give me instructions for the day and reschedule a few appointments before going home but then she sat down for a moment and fell asleep."

"She could not have made the telephone call," Tom murmured.

"Not unless she had an accomplice." In the next breath, Evie changed her mind. "That would require too much planning and something tells me this morning's telephone call was made on the spur of the moment." And something had triggered it, Evie thought.

Had they stumbled on something significant at the jazz club?

They apologized to the young woman. As they walked out of the atelier, they both looked toward the stairs.

Tom adjusted his tie. "I'm surprised you didn't shake Louisa Barclay awake."

"She does have a solid alibi. We can't exactly question it."

"Making that telephone call is the mistake you've been waiting for the killer to make and they will now live to regret it. You have no intention of walking away from this."

She couldn't. Not now.

Evie continued to look toward the stairs. "What are the chances Madame Berger will have an alibi? I still fail to see what the person responsible had to gain by making that telephone call. Although..." Evie shuddered. "What if it had nothing to do with getting us out of the way? What if they wanted to warn us to stop prodding for information or suffer the consequences?" Evie gave her sleeve a firm tug and headed for the stairs.

"I guess you're about to storm in and shoot from the hip."

"I believe we should have listened to Henrietta and forced everyone to tell the truth."

"I'm almost afraid to think what tactics Henrietta might have been prepared to employ."

Evie's steps slowed. "Why did we assume the killer wanted to get us out of the way?"

"Don't beat yourself up about it. You're only trying to make sense of their actions."

Evie's shoulders lowered slightly. "I think we need to use a different method of interrogation with Madame Berger."

"What do you have in mind?"

"I'm not sure, but we should ease into the conversation."

"Would you like me to remind you of that when you go straight for the jugular?"

"I will remain calm." Although, a part of her still raged. How dare someone think they could use Seth to get to her?

Telling herself the detective would be doing everything in his power to get to the bottom of that telephone call went a long way toward calming her.

"Let's do this."

The sound of several people stomping their way up the stairs had them both turning to look down.

Lotte, Caro and Millicent were rushing up the stairs. They were so intent on reaching their destination, they had their eyes to the ground and nearly collided with Tom and Evie.

Caro saw them first. "Milady! Mr. Winchester!"

"Caro. What in heaven's name are you doing here?" Evie asked.

Lotte stopped and bent down at the waist to try to catch her breath.

"We're on a rescue mission, milady."

"Who needs rescuing?"

"The dowagers and Toodles, of course. When we returned from Margaret Thornbury's office, we found Edgar pacing and talking to himself. It took some doing, but he eventually explained the dowagers and Toodles had decided to take matters into their own hands. Especially after... Oh, heavens! Seth. Edgar told us about the telephone call. Actually, the detective told us about it first.... To think, there we were pretending to be applying for a position at Margaret Thornbury's magazine and you were dashing to Seth's rescue."

"He's fine, Caro, and the local constabulary is making sure he remains fine."

"I would feel much better if you'd said he is in excellent health or, at least, safe."

"He's safe."

"But not in excellent health? Has something happened to him, after all?"

"No, Caro. He is both safe and in excellent health."

Caro pressed her hands to her chest. "One of these days, milady, I'm sure you will give me a heart attack."

Lotte straightened. "We really should go up now."

"Oh, yes." Caro gave a vigorous nod. "Edgar said Henrietta had been quite determined to shake the truth out of Madame Berger."

Evie glanced at Tom. "We'd just been wondering what tactics to use with Madame Berger. But... Are you sure they came here?"

"Yes, milady. Edmonds is outside with the Duesenberg."

Lotte cleared her throat and pointed up.

"Yes, of course." Taking a hold of Tom's arm, they set off up the stairs. "I wonder what the detective is doing? I hope he's found a lead. Surely, there must be some way to find out where the telephone call was made." Even if the person responsible had taken care to use another telephone, they would have been seen by someone. "I realize his priority is to find Jacinta McKay's killer but I'm sure this is related."

"The detective is already looking into it," Lotte assured her. "We paid him a visit after we left Margaret Thornbury's office. That's when he told us about Seth and we rushed to your house. Anyhow, he'd just been about to set off to follow a lead. He wouldn't say what it was, but he looked excited."

That sounded promising. "And did your visit to Margaret Thornbury yield any results?"

Lotte nodded. "She isn't dealing well with the crisis at hand. It seems Jacinta played a large role in putting together the magazine. In the time I sat down with her, she had three full glasses of brandy."

Evie found that odd. The magazine owner had come across as being quite capable and in full command of the situation.

The more she thought about it, the more she realized how wrong she'd been about everyone she'd met.

CHAPTER 23

Every step Evie took felt weighed down by denial. The dowagers and Toodles were in no danger. They couldn't be.

She had no idea where this false sense of security came from. Her privileged life did not exempt her from danger or disaster. Yet she held on to her confidence. In this instance, at least, she believed the dowagers and Toodles would take every possible care to ensure they retained the upper hand and remained safe. They had walked into a situation fully prepared to face the worst.

"We can't all barge in there together." Evie looked over her shoulder in time to see Caro's disappointment at her for even suggesting it. Clearly, Caro wanted to get her share of the action.

Prompted by Caro's elbow jab, Millicent drew her eyebrows down and frowned. "Milady, what if Madame Berger is the vicious killer? You'll need our help. Besides, we wouldn't dream of letting you go in there alone. Mr. Winchester might be distracted and then what would you do?"

Glancing at Tom, Evie saw his eyes widen with surprise. "I think you've hurt Mr. Winchester's feelings."

Millicent sniffed. "You never know. I hear there are women who model the clothes and they are very fetching."

Lotte pushed her way to the door. "While you decide what to do, perhaps I should go in and make sure no one's been poisoned."

"What nonsense. Tom and I will go in first. Even if she's guilty, Madame Berger wouldn't dare make such a foolish mistake. If anything, we might have to rescue her from Henrietta's clutches." Despite her determination, Evie made no move to go in.

So far, everyone had provided alibis for that morning so none of them could be responsible for the telephone call. What possible reason could Madame Berger have for scaring Evie half to death? Evie had known her for several years. Heavens, she had come to her rescue. Even if she had been involved in Jacinta's death, why would she want to cause Evie such grief?

"Begging your pardon, milady. Anyone would think you want the dowager to try her best."

"Yes, well... Everyone deserves a moment in the sun."

They all leaned toward the door. Then, one by one, they pressed their ears against it.

"I don't hear anything," Caro whispered.

"This is actually starting to feel suspicious." What if

something had happened to the dowagers and Toodles? "Let's... Let's proceed with care."

Fighting off the urge to burst in, Evie eased the door open and they all piled inside.

Unlike their previous visits, they were not met by Lucy, the receptionist.

Tom whispered, "This makes me realize how little I know about Henrietta. What exactly is she capable of? Do you keep any hunting rifles in the town house?"

"No, and thank goodness for that. I've heard say Henrietta was a crack shot in her youth."

They moved across the reception area toward the door leading to the large salon where they'd previewed Madame Berger's collection.

"This silence is unsettling," Evie murmured.

She wanted to suggest someone should go fetch the police but the next steps brought them all to the door which stood ajar. To her surprise, she saw Henrietta seated by the fireplace sipping a cup of tea.

Giving the door a nudge provided them with a full view of the scene.

Toodles and Sara were seated next to Henrietta and they too were enjoying cups of tea.

Madame Berger and Lucy stood opposite the dowagers and Toodles. While everyone else who worked for Madame Berger stood behind her.

"Oh, Evangeline and... everyone. Do come in and join us," Henrietta invited.

Evie rushed toward the trio. "The tea. You shouldn't be drinking it."

"Nonsense. It's quite safe. Madame Berger would not dream of poisoning us." Lowering her voice,

Henrietta added, "I see you are quite surprised by our presence here. We could no longer sit by doing nothing so we came to accuse her of making that dreadful telephone call and of poisoning Jacinta McKaye."

"And?" Evie couldn't begin to imagine the scene.

"She's quite innocent. As we arrived, the police were leaving. Apparently, they spent the morning doing yet another thorough search of her premises. All the staff were directed to stand right where they are now. So, you see, no one could have made the telephone call."

Evie found herself at a loss for words. What now? With Madame Berger in the clear, they had no more suspects.

Toodles set her teacup down. "Don't worry, Birdie. We've been discussing it and we have decided we'll make our way down the building. I believe Louisa Barclay is next."

"Oh, you needn't bother. Tom and I have already paid her a visit."

"What about Adele Lawson?" Sara asked, her voice edged with a hint of outrage.

"She's also in the clear." Although, Evie remained intrigued by the fact she could hear murmured conversations wafting down from the floors above. "I'm afraid it will be up to the detective now."

Madame Berger cleared her throat and cast a worried look around but didn't say anything.

Henrietta stood up. "Well, I think we have done our duty and I am as disappointed as everyone seems to be at not finding the culprit. Clearly we cannot make any progress here."

Sidling up to Evie, Caro asked, "What now, milady? We can't just leave it at that."

"We'll figure something out, Caro."

Making their way out of the salon, Evie heard a collective sigh from Madame Berger and her staff which prompted her to ask, "Henrietta, how did you get them to cooperate. They looked as if you put the fear of God into them."

Henrietta gave her a triumphant smile. "I invoked the powers that be and used my connection with the Queen."

"Pardon?"

Henrietta's smile widened. "I told Madame Berger I came here on an unofficial capacity but with royal approval."

"You have the Queen's approval?"

"Well, that goes without saying. I would never take it upon myself to misrepresent Her Majesty. However, it is all open to interpretation. Would the Queen wish me to act on her behalf to ensure a possible killer is brought to justice? Yes, indeed."

Evie drew in a calming breath. "Henrietta."

"Her Majesty the Queen has a fascinating ability to know what's what, who's who and who is getting up to what..."

Evie gave her a pointed look.

"Yes, well... She will know I came here, as soon as I tell her. I'm sure she'll find it all very amusing."

When they walked past Louisa Barclay's door, Toodles nudged her. "Are you sure we don't need to have a word with her? I believe Sara has worked herself up into quite a state and she needs to let off some steam."

Evie cast a worried look at the door. Louise Barclay had such a credible, air-tight alibi, Evie knew talking with her would be a waste of time.

Regardless, her imagination took over and she pictured Louisa Barclay organizing someone else to make the telephone call and then deliberately giving herself an alibi by spending the night in prison. Then she remembered Lotte had been responsible for alerting the detective about the drug activities at the jazz club so Louisa could not have known for sure the police would raid the place and take her into custody.

Then again, Louisa had certainly had the means. She knew how to procure the cocaine and buying the poison would have been even easier. Did she have motive? In Evie's opinion, everyone in Jacinta's immediate orbit shared the same motive; they might have been targeted next by Jacinta McKay. They'd also had opportunity to tamper with the cocaine before giving it to Jacinta.

They went down another flight of stairs and as they walked past Adele Lawson's salon, the door opened and she stepped out. Her eyes were still red from crying. Seeing Evie, she choked back an exclamation and hurried back inside where the crying began all over again.

"Of course, they could all be in on it," Evie whispered and considered the possibility of a mass conspiracy to do away with Jacinta McKay.

"Pardon?" Tom asked.

"Oh, nothing." The idea sounded too far-fetched to share. However, there might be a conspiracy of silence. If the killer had any influence, the others might be compelled to keep quiet.

Stepping out of the building, Evie looked at Lotte. Margaret Thornbury had been one of the first people she and Tom had spoken with but they hadn't had as many questions to ask as they did now.

"Did Margaret Thornbury say anything about the canceled advertisements?"

"When I brought up the subject, she brushed it off saying it should all be sorted out soon."

Did that mean she expected Jacinta's death would put a stop to it?

Tom walked straight to the roadster, tipped his hat back and held the door open for her.

Evie hesitated.

She hated the idea of giving up now, but what choice did they have?

"Are we returning to the town house?" Henrietta asked.

"Yes, I think we've had enough excitement for one day." Excitement. Fear. Dread...

They had done everything they could.

And yet, Evie couldn't leave it alone.

Turning to Lotte again, she said, "We'll be returning to Halton House soon. Please join us for dinner tonight."

The invitation drew interested looks from Toodles and the dowagers who were no doubt still keen to see Evie make a commitment to becoming a lady detective.

Everyone made their way to their respective motor cars. Settling into the passenger seat, Evie released a weary sigh.

"Where to?" Tom asked.

The fact he had asked suggested he wasn't quite willing to let go of the investigation either.

She looked up at the building. "We didn't even discover who contacted the police with a story about me having an argument with Jacinta McKay. Heavens, I wouldn't be surprised if she'd made the telephone call herself. But that's not the worst of it. I would have liked to get my hands on the person responsible for fabricating a story about Seth's accident. In fact, if I could only have one wish fulfilled, that would be it."

Tom responded by saying, "They're all waiting for us to make a move."

"Pardon?"

He pointed toward the Duesenberg which was parked across the street and then to Lotte's motor car behind them.

Turning, Evie saw Caro seated on the front passenger seat, her expression downcast.

Evie straightened. "I think we need to go home."

Looking less than thrilled, Tom drove off at a sedate pace. Evie kept her gaze straight ahead, but she caught glimpses of him glancing at her in a way that suggested he might be waiting for her to change her mind.

After a few turns, they were back on Regent Street. Evie crossed her arms and became overwhelmed by a feeling of frustration and resentment followed by renewed outrage that someone could sink so low and, quite possibly, get away with it.

They'd spoken with everyone involved and, from the start, they'd known people had been lying or doing their best to avoid telling the truth.

"Who put on the most convincing act?" she blurted out.

Surprised by the question, Tom gave it some thought and then said, "From the start, Madame Berger displayed nothing but indifference."

Evie agreed. "Yet she said she'd been greatly upset by the experience. Adele Lawson came across as quite levelheaded, but when we applied the slightest pressure, she broke down."

Tom managed to lighten the mood by saying, "We? I believe that was all your doing. I prefer not to make women cry."

"Not even if you suspect them of using a child as a decoy?" What had been the point of doing that? No one had used the opportunity to flee. "I think we're dealing with a very sick mind." Someone who enjoyed seeing people suffer, she thought. "Then, there's Louisa Barclay. She just happened to be in the right place and served as a witness, corroborating Madame Berger's story. We didn't notice anything unusual about her but then I had the encounter with her at the jazz club." Evie fell silent. Her back teeth ground together. A feeling of rage surged through her with renewed intensity.

No, she couldn't let it go.

They would simply have to start at the beginning and work their way from one suspect to the next. There had to be something they'd missed.

Something in plain sight. Something obvious.

Evie turned her thoughts to motive. This time, however, she focused on Jacinta's motive.

Why had she written the derogatory article?

Margaret Thornbury had told them Jacinta had been fully responsible for writing whatever she liked.

Evie straightened. Her thoughts stalled and then jump-started again.

"That was the biggest lie of them all." Pointing to a side street, Evie directed Tom to make a turn.

"Where are we going?"

"To have another chat with Margaret Thornbury," she growled.

Tom got them moving and after a moment he turned to her. "We have company."

A quick glance over her shoulder had Evie smiling. They were being followed by the Duesenberg with Lotte not far behind.

"What's on your mind, Countess?"

Evie spoke through gritted teeth, "I have decided Margaret Thornbury put on the best act. The more I think about it, the more I believe she's involved. Yes, indeed. She is at the heart of it." Evie straightened. "Regardless of what she said, Jacinta worked for her. Editors always have the last say on everything."

"Strange," Tom mused. "I thought you might have had second thoughts about Adele Lawson. I still can't believe how she fell to pieces. That could easily have been the best performance."

Evie gasped.

"What?"

"When you telephoned the detective from Seth's school he told you he'd been talking with Adele Lawson. When she became upset, she said she'd told him everything."

"That's right."

"Are we missing something? What exactly did she say to him?" Adele had wailed the words out. Had Adele's emphatic admission suggested she had finally broken down and revealed everything she'd known?

"The detective didn't go into details," Tom said.

"Earlier, Lotte said he'd been on the way out to follow a lead. This happened right after he interviewed Adele Lawson. She must have given him information she'd been withholding."

"Do you want me to turn around?"

As much as she wished to know exactly what Adele had told the detective, she insisted they needed to talk with Margaret Thornbury first. She'd fooled them with a convincing act, one she hadn't managed to keep up. What had driven her to drink? Why had she gone off the rails?

"No. Keep going."

Tom maneuvered the motor car through the busy street and made another turn. As they approached the building housing Margaret Thornbury's magazine, they both leaned forward.

"Is that the police going into the building?" Evie asked.

Her mind raced. Excitement pumped through her.

What had the detective discovered?

Evie slumped back on her seat and as she stared straight ahead, all the pieces began to fall into place.

Soon after taking some cocaine, Jacinta must have known something was wrong. She had made her way up to Madame Berger's salon.

She'd wanted to warn her. She would be next...

Evie pressed her hands against her cheek. Without realizing it, Jacinta had pointed to her killer.

The moment the motor car came to a stop, she jumped out and rushed toward the building with Tom following only a few steps behind.

When he caught up to her, she said, "Despite what she said, Margaret Thornbury directed Jacinta to write the article. The clue was there from the start."

"This is about Jacinta's remark."

"Yes. Of course she wasn't going to accept responsibility. It hadn't been her decision."

"But why? What reason did Margaret Thornbury have for wanting to destroy Madame Berger's reputation?"

Evie went through all the possible reasons and focused on revenge. "Madame Berger must have done something... or said something." Evie clicked her fingers and nearly missed a step. Luckily, Tom caught her in time and steadied her. With her breath coming hard and fast, she said, "What if someone overheard Madame Berger..."

"Saying what?"

"Oh, heavens. The chimney. And... I don't know... She said something. A secret. A rumor about Margaret Thornbury. Adele Lawson might have heard it and it somehow got back to Margaret Thornbury. Or maybe, just maybe, Jacinta had been visiting Adele and she heard a conversation wafting down the chimney the way we did. She then reported back to Margaret Thornbury and received instructions to pay Madame Berger back with a bad review."

She expected Tom to laugh at her overactive imagination. Instead, he nodded.

"It would justify Jacinta's remark."

"Even if I've been talking nothing but nonsense, we must be on the right track. Otherwise, why would the police be here?"

As they reached the first floor, Evie turned to take the next step leading to Margaret's apartment but Tom grabbed her arm and pulled her back.

He put his finger to his lips and whispered, "I just caught sight of a policeman. I think she might be in the office."

They both looked around the corner and then plastered themselves against the wall.

"What now?" Tom mouthed.

Evie whispered against his ear, "The detective followed a lead *after* he spoke with Adele Lawson. She told him something she didn't tell us. It must have led him straight to Margaret Thornbury."

Evie growled under her breath. Why had she killed Jacinta? Had she threatened to expose Margaret?

Evie remembered the detective mentioning money. Had Jacinta been blackmailing Margaret Thornbury?

Squaring her shoulders, she scurried toward the office.

Tom tried to grab her and pull her back, but he missed by a mere inch.

Margaret Thornbury.

She had to be behind all this...

CHAPTER 24

Evie rounded the corner, stormed past the policeman standing near the door and barged into the office.

She could see several people but her eyes targeted only one person. Margaret Thornbury.

Evie marched straight up to her, drew her fist back and released it with the full force of her pent-up anger.

As the moment registered in her mind, she sprung back and cupped her hand against her chest.

"Lady Woodridge!" someone exclaimed.

Then, Evie heard a chorus of other voices.

"Milady!"

"Evangeline!"

"Birdie!"

"Countess!"

"Oh, my. Evie... Well done."

Turning slightly, Evie saw Sara smiling, her eyes brimming with pride.

The dowagers, Toodles, Lotte, Caro and Millicent

had followed her and Tom into the building and had clearly seen her brazen act of shoot first and ask questions later.

Tom stood behind them, his look of utter disbelief interrupted only when the policeman gave his arm a tug. It seemed he'd only been able to stop Tom, while the others had scrambled past him.

Evie rubbed her sore hand.

In her mind, her action had been self-explanatory. However, she hoped she wouldn't be asked to justify herself because, even now, she struggled to make sense of the instinct that had driven her to attack Margaret Thornbury.

Turning back to the scene in front of her, she saw the editor of The Stylist clutching her nose. A second later, she sent Evie a murderous look and emitted a loud wail.

Evie stood her ground. Come what may, she would not apologize.

Out of the corner of her eye, Evie saw someone approaching. The detective.

"Lady Woodridge," he said in a calm tone.

Belatedly, she realized the detective had been the first person to express his surprise.

Evie glanced down at her hand and then straightened. "Detective. I suppose you wish to know what I'm doing here."

"That is one question I would like to hear you answer, but I'm more curious to know why you assaulted my suspect."

"Aha! So she is a suspect." Thank goodness, Evie thought.

Henrietta stepped up. "Inspector, I hope you are not thinking of taking Evangeline into custody. She must have had a very good reason for doing what she did."

The detective signaled to the police constable. "I think Margaret Thornbury needs medical attention."

The constable, who had been holding on to Tom, released him and made his way to the telephone.

Another constable stepped up and went to stand beside Margaret Thornbury while the detective ushered everyone out of the office and into the foyer.

"Are you going to keep us in the dark?" Henrietta asked.

"He wouldn't dare," Sara exclaimed.

"Did Adele Lawson have something to do with you being here?" Evie asked.

The detective slipped his hands inside his pockets and looked down at the ground. "I hope you realize I could have you all escorted out of the building."

Henrietta scoffed at the idea.

He turned to Evie. "In answer to your question, my lady, yes, Adele Lawson came through with some vital information. You were on the right track. She overheard a conversation."

"From the chimney?"

"Yes. Jacinta McKay had been with her and she reported back to Margaret Thornbury."

Evie's mind filled with possibilities. "What did they hear?"

"A rumor about Margaret Thornbury's husband. He died in a riding accident, or so it seems."

"She poisoned him!"

"We are still investigating. From what we have

discovered, Margaret Thornbury wanted a divorce and her husband refused to give it to her. Anyhow, after hearing about the rumor, she instructed Jacinta to write the article to punish Madame Berger. Then, Jacinta decided to blackmail Margaret Thornbury."

Henrietta's eyes brightened. "And Margaret Thornbury poisoned her."

"She will have a hard time explaining the poison we found in her apartment, as well as the cocaine and the fact she had withdrawn the exact amount we found in Jacinta's possession."

"Well done, Countess."

Evie pushed past the pain and smiled at Tom who came to stand beside her to inspect her hand. "Did you keep your thumb out?"

Evie grinned. "Yes."

"Well, there's nothing broken."

The detective cleared his throat. "How am I going to explain this?"

"Oh, never mind all that. Why was everyone so secretive, especially Adele?" Evie asked. "Did they fear Margaret Thornbury's reprisal?"

"It would appear so." The detective crossed his arms. "Would you mind telling me how you came to believe her to be guilty?"

"I'm afraid I did not rely on any hard evidence. Jacinta McKay made a comment which basically pointed the finger at her employer. It's been puzzling me from the start but I couldn't make any sense of it. I believe she made her way up to Madame Berger's salon to warn her."

"Unfortunately, we will never know for sure. I can,

however, tell you the telephone exchange was able to confirm Margaret Thornbury made a telephone call to your house." He looked up at the ceiling. "Perhaps we can use that to justify your actions. Also, while Margaret Thornbury is denying any involvement, she did say Adele Lawson was the one who offered the account to the police about seeing you having an altercation. Adele Lawson swears she acted on Margaret Thornbury's instructions." He glanced toward the office. "The more she talks, the less sense she makes. I think there might be something quite wrong with her."

Evie rubbed her hand. "I should think so. How did she explain placing that telephone call? There was simply no need for it."

"I'm afraid she has taken a dislike to you. The more I think about it, the more I believe there is something wrong with her."

Evie exchanged a look with Tom. Earlier, they had both concluded the person responsible for the telephone call had to be truly evil.

Henrietta shook her head. "Well, I hope you will lock her up and throw away the key."

"You should have that hand looked at, my lady."

Evie took the prompt as a warning to vacate the premises. While she hurried away, Caro and Millicent lagged behind. Urged by Tom to follow them out of the building, her maids harrumphed.

"It's not fair that we didn't get to have a shot at that woman."

"Caro! I'm sure Mrs. Mannering will be the first to say you should avoid any such transgressions. Such behavior is unprofessional. I'm sorry you witnessed it. I really don't wish you to feel we are free to take such actions."

"But you did and I'm sure you're not sorry you did, milady."

"Yes, well... Never mind all that. I think we could all do with a strong cup of tea. Or, better still, a Birdie."

EPILOGUE

Evie glanced at the day's headlines and turned the page over.

Margaret Thornbury's trial had been scheduled but with so much solid evidence against her, she didn't stand a chance of ever seeing freedom again.

Dubbed the Fashion House Murder, newspaper reporters had been having a field day...

"And forgetting all about me," Evie murmured and continued to search Martin Gate's newspaper for the retraction he had promised.

Henrietta's cheers drew Evie's attention to the game of cricket in progress. They had taken Seth out of school for the day and had settled on the banks of a nearby river to enjoy their lunch.

"I think Tom's technique needs some work." When Seth sent the ball flying across the river bank, Henrietta clapped. "Oh, well done, Seth."

Evie watched Caro and Millicent running after the

ball and Seth holding up his bat in triumph as he made another run.

Smiling, she turned the page of the newspaper and resumed skimming through it.

"More tea, my lady?" Edgar asked.

"Thank you, Edgar."

Evie turned the next page.

"Birdie," Toodles called out from the field. "You must take a turn throwing the ball."

Evie held her hand up. "I'm still injured, Grans." She watched Tom deliver the next ball. Seth struck it cleanly and made several runs. Satisfied, she returned to her newspaper.

"Evie, you should try some of this lemon cake." Sara leaned forward and selected a piece for her.

Evie hummed under her breath. If she didn't know better, she'd say everyone had conspired to draw her attention away from the newspaper...

Her gaze landed on a column of no more than a couple of dozen words. As she read, her lips parted.

Out of the corner of her eye, she saw Henrietta nudging Sara.

"Your tea is getting cold, Evangeline."

"Are you sure you don't want some cake?" Sara asked. "It's truly divine."

Evie pointed an accusatory finger at the article that had caught her eye. "The Countess of Woodridge and Mr. Tom Winchester will make a formal announcement as soon as they have gained the head of the household's permission? They are rumored to be spending the day with the current Earl of Woodridge, seven-year-old Seth Halton..."

"Oh," Henrietta exclaimed.

"Was that a question or a statement?" Sara asked.

Gasping for breath, Evie demanded, "H-how did Martin Gate come by this information?"

"Well, he knew of your engagement," Henrietta mused.

"My fake engagement."

"Oh," Sara exclaimed. "It sounded real enough to us."

"Meaning?"

The dowagers exchanged a look of mischief.

Shrugging, Sara said, "From what we understand, the ingredients for a cake are being gathered. You know how difficult they still are to obtain. And, you did place an order for a dress with Adele Lawson."

Henrietta nodded. "Yes. A beige dress. Oh, dear. I hope you haven't changed your mind about the color. We have already coordinated our gowns..."

Evie set the newspaper down. "I take it you have all decided on a date? And my question still stands. How did Martin Gate come by this information?"

A round of applause drew everyone's attention back to the game, which had now ended. Toodles, Millicent and Caro were headed their way while Tom and Seth walked several paces behind them, deep in conversation...

"It seems we have a mystery on our hands," Henrietta said.

"More like an informer," Evie muttered.

"Well, I for one, welcome the news," Henrietta declared. "It is just the sort of diversion we need to take everyone's mind off that dreadful photograph they printed of us at the jazz club..."

"I see. So, now I'm supposed to go ahead with the nuptials just so you can have some peace of mind?"

Henrietta grinned. "Oh, that would be ever so considerate of you, Evangeline. Of course, if you turned your attention to becoming a lady detective, you will have to postpone your wedding... Then again, what are the chances of someone within your vicinity being murdered and taking your focus away from the wedding preparations?"

Evie slanted her gaze. "They are looking quite good at the moment..."

Sara leaned forward and discreetly moved the butter knife away from Evie's reach...

Before she could say anything, Seth came trotting up to them. "Cousin Evie. I believe congratulations are in order..."

Printed in Great Britain
by Amazon